ABANDONED WHARF SISTERS

Victorian Romance

FAYE GODWIN

Tica House Publishing

Sweet Romance that Delights and Enchants!

Copyright © 2020 by Faye Godwin

All rights reserved.

No part of this book may be reproduced in any form or by any electronic or mechanical means, including information storage and retrieval systems, without written permission from the author, except for the use of brief quotations in a book review.

PERSONAL WORD FROM THE AUTHOR

Dearest Readers,

I'm so delighted that you have chosen one of my books to read. I am proud to be a part of the team of writers at Tica House Publishing. Our goal is to inspire, entertain, and give you many hours of reading pleasure. Your kind words and loving readership are deeply appreciated.

I would like to personally invite you to sign up for updates and to become part of our **Exclusive Reader Club**—it's completely Free to Join! I'd love to welcome you!

Much love,

Faye Godwin

VISIT HERE to Join our Reader's Club and to Receive Tica House Updates:

https://victorian.subscribemenow.com/

PART I

CHAPTER 1

IT HAD BEEN another long Friday at the Billingsgate fish market, and Effie was beginning to wonder if she would ever smell like anything other than fish again. Her feet ached from hours of standing behind a stall, and she was beginning to feel as stiff and dead-eyed as the cod and haddock that she'd been trying to sell to the heedless masses of the public.

She wrapped her arms more tightly around herself as she walked through the streets of Whitechapel, trying to make herself invisible to the men on the street corners with darting dark eyes. A pony and cart rattled past, and Effie averted her eyes. She knew there was only one kind of cart that came down here, and it was the undertaker's. She didn't want to see what was on the back of that cart. Instead, she fixed her eyes on the ground, watching her feet carry her across the frozen mud, sidestepping the odd suspicious rag or dead rat. The smell of fish was overpowering, but perhaps that wasn't such a bad thing. Whitechapel sometimes smelt even worse.

The further Effie walked, the more crowded the narrow streets become. Precarious houses built of wood and bricks leaned over the street like they were scrutinizing her, their broken windows making them look gap-toothed and staring. She tucked her thin shawl a little more closely around herself, glancing up at the sky. It was the palest blue, almost gray, and she knew that sunset was coming soon. She had to be back home before then. The cold was already bitter and brutal; the tip of Effie's nose was numb, and every hasty breath came out steaming. But when that sun went down, it would be intolerable.

At last, Effie turned the corner, and there it was – the third building on the left, an ugly thing that hunched miserably between its glowering neighbors. The wall was cracked dangerously on one side and many of the walls had holes in them, but it was somewhere that she could rest, at least. Somewhere that she could get dry and warm. Effie broke into a jog at the sight of her tenement building. The front door creaked when she touched it; she had to be careful how she swung it open so that its dodgy hinge didn't pop right off. Her footsteps echoed in the long, dark corridor.

"Mama?" Effie called out softly, trying not to wake their neighbor across the hallway, grumpy Mr. Dixon. "Papa?"

There was no reply. She gave the door a gentle push, and

instead of the warm flicker of firelight, she was met with a dull glow that filled the room with shadows. Effie's eyes could only just make out the vague shape of two sleeping pallets, one in each back corner. There was a bucket by the fireplace, a three-legged pot missing one of its legs, a ladle, and nothing much else.

Four little faces looked up at her from one of the sleeping pallets, bundled up in two threadbare blankets. "Effie!" cried the smallest one.

"Hello, love," said Effie. She put down the paper bag of coal and held out her arms as the heap of limbs erupted into three small girls, who ran straight toward her, and a boy who followed a little distance behind. She scooped the smallest of the girls into her arms and smoothed down her red hair. "Effie," said the little girl again, burying her face in Effie's neck. It was warm and cuddly, and Effie cradled her.

"Annie, I also want a turn," piped up a voice from Effie's knees.

"Come on, Sadie," said Effie, holding out her free arm. "Up you get."

Sadie scrambled into her arms, and Effie held them both, leaving her middle sister – Rose – to pout on the floor. "What about me?"

"You have more than one big sibling, you know," said the boy, his tone teasing. He grabbed Rose's arms and swung her up onto his shoulders, making her squeal with glee. "I'm here, too."

"John!" Rose squealed, clinging to her brother's collar.

Effie laughed, putting down the other two girls. "Here," she said, grabbing the paper bag again. "Let's wake this fire up a bit, shall we? It's so cold in here."

"I'll do it," said John, taking the bag. "Did you bring something for supper?"

Effie paused, and their eyes met. The little girls were running to the fire in expectation, their small faces blue with cold. John said nothing, and neither did she, but she read everything in his brown eyes.

"I think we still have a heel of bread," said John quietly. "It's a little stale, but it's something."

Effie tried her best to smile. Sometimes, the world felt much too heavy for her thirteen-year-old shoulders. "The coal was cheaper today," she said. "I've still got tuppence left. It's something. I'll see if I can find something…"

"It's all right," said John. "You've been out in the cold all day. You make the fire, I'll find food."

Effie studied him for a moment. His face was so pale, the skin pinched tight over his high cheekbones. The eyes were full of life, but the bony body looked much older than his eleven years, as though it had to bear the hardships of a lifetime. He was too young to be going out there on his own. Then again, wasn't she?

"Effie, it's all right." John put a hand on her shoulder. "I'll be back before you know it. I'll just run to the old lady with the soup around the corner."

"All right," said Effie reluctantly. She passed him the two shiny little coins, and he clutched them tightly. "Please be safe. And hurry. It's freezing out."

John disappeared, and Effie turned back to the little girls. She worked fast, adding coal to the last flicker of the fire, and by the time John returned there was a small circle of warmth around the fireplace. Effie had bundled the two smallest girls, Rose and Annie, in the blankets and sandwiched Sadie between them, and the color was starting to return to their fingers and faces. John had picked up their little tin pot, and there was steam coming out of it.

"Soup!" gasped the little girls in unison, their eyes widening.

Effie glanced into the pot, knowing immediately that there wasn't enough for her. She smiled at John. "Thanks," she said, taking the pot. Carrot tops and nameless globs of pale meat bumped into each other in the watery mixture.

"That's better," said John, smiling at the little girls. "Let me get the cups out."

He fished five tin cups out of the box that served as their kitchen cupboard and Effie tipped the soup into four of them.

John tried to give her one, but she'd only been able to half fill them as it was, and she pressed the warm cup back into his hand. "I've got the bread," she said brightly. "I'm all right. Mrs. Flanders gave me something to eat at lunchtime."

"She did?" said John dubiously.

"Of course," said Effie. He didn't need to know that it had only been a cup of weak tea and a rusk.

John gave her a doubtful look, but he was too hungry to argue. He perched on the upturned bucket while they ate. The little girls were ravenous; they gulped the hot soup down in shaky movements that jerked with desperation, and it seemed to last only a few seconds before it was all gone. Effie took the cups from them, and they curled up around each other, falling asleep on the hearth in seconds.

John leaned forward, tugging the larger blanket so that it covered both Sadie and Rose. Rose stirred, her knotted brown hair brushing her cheeks, and slipped a thumb into her mouth. She began to suck quietly, and Effie felt as though her heart was being squeezed.

John looked up at her. "At least they've had something to eat," he said softly.

"Yes. They're all right for now," said Effie. "The coal has to last us tomorrow and Sunday, though. Mrs. Flanders will pay me again tomorrow, but it has to go to rent on Monday."

John nodded, and Effie felt the next question yawning at her feet like a bottomless pit. She took a deep breath and touched John's shoulder. "John... where are Mama and Papa?"

John let out a snort that made Annie stir. "Where do you think, Effie?"

"I'm just asking."

"Well, Papa came blundering in here just after you'd left for work," said John. "Completely blootered, as usual, couldn't even stand up straight and reeking of drink. He yelled at the girls until they cried and then fell asleep there on the pallet." He pointed. "Then Mama slapped him awake and told him to go to work, but he didn't. He just sat on the bucket and drank until the bottle was empty. Then she kicked him until he woke up, and they went off."

He spoke mechanically, as if he had less emotion than the looms of the cotton mill where Mama worked. Effie bit her lip, fighting to hold back the tears. She wished Mama and Papa were here, but she wasn't sorry that she hadn't had to put up with them all day.

"They're gone, Effie," said John quietly.

The tone of his voice scared her. "Gone?" said Effie.

"They've left. Don't you see?" John looked up at her, his eyes suddenly deep with tears. "They're not coming back."

"They'll come back. They're just a bit late, as usual," said Effie.

"No, they won't. Not this time." John looked away. "Papa said so."

"Papa was drunk."

"Papa's not coming back, Effie," said John. "Not for a week, or a month, or who knows how long this time." He folded his arms. "And I'm not going to miss them."

Effie put an arm around her younger brother, trying to keep the fear at bay. She knew in her gut that John was right. "We'll be all right, John," she said. "At least I'm used to paying the rent."

"The rent is one thing. Food is another," said John. "How are we going to find it, Effie?" He looked down at the girls, and a shudder ran through him. "How are we going to feed them?" he whispered.

Effie didn't know the answer. She just pulled John closer and rested her forehead on his shoulder, hoping that somehow, they were going to be all right.

CHAPTER 2

A WEEK HAD PASSED, and then another, and every time that Effie walked into the cold and drafty tenement, she clung fiercely to the hope that Mama and Papa were somehow going to reappear, and that every evening they would be there waiting for her. But they weren't.

What met her every evening were John and Rose and Annie and Sadie, huddled by a dying fire, their eyes hollow, their bellies empty.

Snow swirled around Effie, finding all the seams in her clothes and thrusting its cold fingers against her skin as she hurried up to the door of the tenement, clutching a fish wrapped in newspaper to her chest. The customers hadn't liked it because it was floppy instead of firm, and there was a questionable smell coming from it that made Effie wish she hadn't been hugging it to her chest all the way from Billingsgate. Still, Mrs. Flanders had sold it to her for a tenth of the usual price, and it would fill them up well. She pushed the door open, calling out, "Mama?" as hopefully as she could.

"She's not here, Effie," snapped John.

The girls were asleep in a cuddled heap on their pallet. Effie let out a sigh, putting the fish down on the table, which wobbled even at that slight weight. "At least I've brought supper," she said.

"Yes," said John grimly, "but it's no use."

Effie stared at him. "What do you mean?"

"It's the coal." John picked up the bucket, holding it up to Effie. To her dismay, the last of their coal was swimming in water. "There's a new leak in the roof, and it's soaked. We've only got enough for tonight."

Effie passed an exhausted hand over her face, her strength momentarily leaving her. She sagged down onto the nearest pallet. "And I have to pay the rent with tomorrow's wage," she said faintly.

John sat down beside her. He was hugging his knees, looking somehow younger than his eleven years in the set of his shoulders and the curve of his back, but when he looked up at Effie his eyes were filled with a desperation as old as humanity.

"Effie," he said, his tone gentle. He reached over and put a bony arm around her shoulders. "We can't go on like this."

Effie looked up at him, terrified. An image flitted through her mind: a gray image of a stern, pillared building filled with people in ugly uniforms who'd stared at her from the doorway like prisoners or slaves. "No, John, no," she whispered. "Not that. Anything but that."

"I just want to help," said John softly.

"I won't have it!" Effie leaped to her feet. "Not the girls. Not you. No! I won't have you in the workhouse."

"Workhouse?" John shook his head, fear filling his expression. "No, Effie. No. You're right. I don't want that for us either."

Effie's shoulders sagged. "I can't have that happen to you."

"Neither can I. Can you imagine Annie..." John's eyes filled with pain, and he shook his head. "No."

"Then what are we going to do, John?" asked Effie. "I know we can't go on like this. But apart from the workhouse, we have no other choice."

"We do have a choice," said John. "The girls and I spend all day sitting around in the tenement doing nothing. We can go out and do something, too."

"What can you do, John? Sadie's only nine, and she's the oldest."

"I don't know. Maybe we can go and work in a factory."

A shudder crept icily down Effie's spine. "No," she said firmly. "Don't you remember my friend Caroline from when I was little?"

"Caroline? The girl with the black hair?" John frowned. "Didn't she die of cancer?"

"Cancer of the jaw," said Effie. "She got it from working in a match factory."

"Well, then, we'll do something else. We'll go out and beg," said John. "The girls are beautiful if we can get them cleaned up. People will feel sorry for us. They'll give us money, Effie. It'll be something."

"It's so cold, though," said Effie reluctantly.

"Effie." John wrapped both his arms around her and stared up at her imploringly, his eyes bottomless as tar pits. "Please. Let me help. You can't do this all alone."

"No," Effie whispered. She returned John's embrace, clutching his skeletal frame, resting her cheek on the top of his oily head. He was so thin, and his limbs so cold, and she didn't know what to do. "I have to do this all alone," she whispered.

◈

"HERRING!" EFFIE CALLED, HER VOICE SOUNDING THIN AND

reedy against the roaring hubbub of the market. "Good, fresh herring, only a shilling for a dozen! Smelts, two shillings a hundred!" She grasped at a random fish on the table in front of her and heaved it into the air, the slippery object feeling as greasy and quick in her hands as if it was still alive and cleaving the ocean current. "Hey-o!" she shouted, thinly, trying her best to make herself heard. "Lovely live lobsters! Perfect middling size. Delicious for your supper table!"

A portly lady passed just a little closer to her stall than the rest of the crowd, and Effie lunged at her, brandishing a fresh haddock. "Hello, ma'am. How about a lovely bit o' haddock, then? Won't it go down well for your husband?"

The woman gave Effie a dark glare out of beady eyes. "I doubt it," she said. "My husband's been dead these twenty years."

"Oh," said Effie. She lowered the haddock onto the table, and the woman bustled away.

The market was utterly packed with people, stalls, and fish. Effie didn't know how it was possible to feel so lonely amid such a crush of people. They all seemed so happy and alive, and so unworried. There was a young couple strolling by just in front of her, and even though their clothes had often been mended and there was a little hole in the back of the young gentleman's shoe, they seemed the happiest people that Effie had ever seen. They were gazing up at each other as they strolled by hand in hand, the gentleman carrying a battered basket on his arm. They seemed to have so little, and yet so much, their smiles lighting up the whole market.

Effie felt as though they were a completely different species than she was. She looked down at the fish spread out in front of her, and the cold wind rattled the rickety corners of her stall once again, sending little swirls of snowflakes to touch her skin with a deathly kiss. She felt she could relate better to the fish than to the people. Like the fish, she was cold, and stiff, and dead-eyed.

There was a creak from behind her, and Effie turned as old Mrs. Flanders rose from her wooden chair as stiff as a corpse. She even looked like on, possessing a long face with the flesh sagging off her bones like it was about to rot away. "Pack away these things, child," she croaked. "It's time to go home."

Mrs. Flanders' voice had abandoned her a few years ago thanks to years of crying her wares in the noisy market. She hardly ever spoke, but Effie liked her despite her cadaverous appearance, knowing that there was a glint of kindness somewhere underneath it. She nodded and got to work, moving fast. The snow was falling harder now, and the very air itself seemed to have teeth, sinking them like icy needles into the tiniest gap of exposed flesh. John, Rose, Sadie and Annie were out there somewhere in this, and Effie couldn't bear to think of them battling the elements. She prayed that John had had the sense to go back inside before this icy wind arose.

Mrs. Flanders bid her a hurried farewell, shoving a few coins into Effie's palm. She dumped them into the front pocket of her apron without even looking at them and broke into a jog as she hurried back toward Whitechapel as fast as her legs could carry her. It was not just haste that drove her to run: the cold was stalking her now, creeping behind her, clinging to the lengthening shadows like a vengeful wolf pack on the prowl. Running seemed the only way to keep it at bay, and even though her feet hurt and her legs ached and her chest burned when she ran for too long. Still, it was better than feeling that insidious cold seep into her body.

When she hastened up the hallway of the tenement, it was hardly better inside. The wind howled through the broken windowpanes and the gaps in the bricks and the holes in the doors, and it brought little scatterings of snowflakes with it. Effie tried to make herself walk, not wanting to frighten the children. But when she saw that the door to their room was open, she couldn't help it. She lunged inside.

It was Sadie. She stood in front of the fire, her lips utterly blue, goosebumps peppering her body as Rose and Annie struggled to help her pull off her dress, which was soaked through. There was a pool of frigid water lying on the floor around Sadie's feet, and her hair was sodden. John was crouched by the fire, blowing it to life, his own body trembling uncontrollably.

"Sadie!" Effie cried. She slammed the door behind her and ran to help, pulling the soaked linen over Sadie's head. It dripped in her hands; she threw it on the ground and grabbed a blanket, wrapping it around the little girl's body. "What on earth happened?"

"It wasn't his fault, Effie," cried Rose. "Please, don't be angry with us."

"I'm not angry." Effie took a deep breath, trying her best to control the terror bubbling up inside her. "I just want to know what happened."

"It was a cart," Sadie stammered out between chattering teeth. "We were walking home past the brewery and they'd just been pumping water and there was a big cold puddle freezing over in front of it. And then all these young gentlemen came driving past as fast as they could in a hansom."

"Fools!" snapped John. "Nanty-narking about while some of us don't have anything to eat." He gave the fire a furious prod with the poker. "They sent up a huge splash of water. It soaked Sadie to the bone. We had to run home, or her clothes would have frozen to her."

"Oh, Sadie." Effie wrapped her arms around the little girl, holding her tightly. "You poor thing."

"I'm all right, sis," said Sadie courageously. "Just a little cold."

Effie tried her best to smile, forcing down her own rising tears. "Yes, you're all right, darling," she said, knowing in her heart that her words weren't true. Cold wasn't just cold; Effie knew that they were all just one soaking away from consumption. "Come – sit down."

She settled Sadie on the bare hearth, tucking both their blankets securely around the child's shoulders, and hurried to serve her some of the watery broth that she'd made the night before from some chicken gizzards. Effie had added so much water to it that was little more than water with a few bits of turnip, and certainly no flavor, but Sadie choked it down fast.

"I'm sorry, Effie," said John softly as they watched her blowing on the hot soup.

Effie didn't know what to say. John reached into his pocket and pulled out a few coins. "Here," he said. "At least, it's something."

Effie looked down at the money he'd pressed into her palm. It was so cold and dead in her hands, yet she knew that they needed it.

She looked back up at Sadie. Did they really need it this much?

***

It was still quite dark when Effie opened her eyes. The cold was running its fingers over her shoulder even though she'd gone to bed wearing all the clothing she owned, which wasn't much: her tattered dress, a jumper with holes in it, a coat that might have been quite fine once. She stirred on the hard pallet, feeling out all the aches and bruises the night's rest had given her, and wrapped her arms more securely around little Annie. The child slept peacefully, her head resting on Effie's shoulder, the shock of red hair blooming over the ragged blanket. Behind Effie, Rose was curled up against the small of her back.

She glanced over at the other pallet. Sadie was sleeping soundly; her face didn't look blue anymore, and John was holding her protectively, his skinny arm draped over her body. Effie sat up as gently as she could, letting Annie roll over and clutch Rose, and tucked the blanket back around the girls. She crossed the floor and knelt by the other sleeping pallet. "John," she whispered, touching her brother's shoulders.

He was awake immediately, deep eyes wide as he looked up at her. He glanced down at Sadie, his arm tightening around her. The little girl stirred, and Effie touched her cheek. It wasn't hot. "She's all right, John," she said. "But I need to talk to you."

John nodded mutely. He slipped off of the pallet, also wearing all his clothes, and followed Effie as she wiped her face with some murky water and tried to tug the worst of the tangles out of her hair in the firelight. It only took a few minutes. Soon they were outside the door, safely out of earshot of the three little ones, and Effie closed the door softly behind them.

"What is it?" asked John.

"John…" Effie put a hand on his shoulder, wishing he didn't

have to grow up so fast. "Thanks for everything you're doing with trying to make money for us, but I don't want you to go out begging with the girls anymore."

John stepped back. "It was an accident, Effie. That cart came by so fast, and..."

"I know," Effie said quickly. "I understand, and it wasn't your fault. But the winter is bitter out there, Johnny. The papers are all saying that it's breaking records. It's so cold. The girls are going to catch their deaths... and so are you." She shook her head. "I can't let that happen."

"Would you have us starve, then?" demanded John.

"I don't know what I'd have us do. But you can't go outside," said Effie, her tone growing firmer. "Please, John. Don't fight me on this. Don't go begging with the girls anymore."

"Then I'll go alone," said John fiercely.

"No!" Effie didn't mean to snap, but it came out that way. She took a deep breath, trying to calm herself. "No. Don't do that. Please don't leave them alone. I can't bear to think of them being without you."

John relented. His dark eyes studied hers. "We need the money," he said softly.

"I know we do. But I'll think of another way." Effie put both hands on his shoulders, gripping them tightly, feeling how thin his skin was against his small bones. "John, I need you to promise me that you won't take the girls out of this tenement."

John looked away, the set of his mouth turning bitter.

"I promise," he muttered.

Effie hoped she could trust John's word. She hated that she had even a flicker of doubt about him, but something about the way he'd looked away as he spoke made a strange little snake of distrust curl and writhe in her stomach. She tried to ignore it, wrapping her arms more securely around herself, walking as fast as she could toward the fish market. Her breath was curling in the air around her, and she kept her fingers pushed up into her sleeves. She couldn't cover her nose, though, and the cold air snapped at it with icy fangs.

The fog was impenetrable. It hung between the houses of Whitechapel like a stage curtain, masking the familiar shapes of the buildings until they were stretched and tortured into the howling visages of looming monsters. Effie tried not to look at them but looking ahead was hardly any better; the fog was so thick that she couldn't see to the end of the street. It felt as though she might walk off the very edge of the world if she kept going.

Her feet bore her to Billingsgate at last, but Effie knew it was going to be a quiet day before she even stepped into the empty market square. Anyone with any sense, she thought – or anyone whose home was more than just a frozen shell – would be safely tucked away in their houses rather than braving the fog to go out and buy fish. She imagined a crackling fireplace and warm, thick curtains and a woolly rug that was soft and deep on her feet. The images were filled with longing. She'd looked through the windows of houses like that, but she had no idea what it was really like to be warm every night.

Mrs. Flanders was waiting for her, packing out the fish on the table. There was no need to try to keep them cool; the air was so cold that they were almost freezing where they lay. "Morning, Mrs. Flanders," said Effie.

Mrs. Flanders smiled and squeezed the words out of her exhausted voice. "Morning," she said.

Effie helped to set up the stall and pack out the fish, checking on the live crabs and lobsters that were floating around in their cistern. They were a little small, and there were only four crabs and two lobsters left. She hoped that Mrs. Flanders' son would be able to head out over the icy Thames again soon and bring some fresh catch. What if Mrs. Flanders didn't sell fish anymore? She wouldn't have a job. She wouldn't be able to feed the children. She wouldn't know what to…

"Effie?"

Effie looked up from the cistern. A familiar, broad, freckled face smiled at her from the other side of the table, and a rush of delight warmed her heart. "Willie!" she said. "It's been so long."

"I know." Willie laughed, a rich, full sound, warm as the color of old brown sherry. His eyes were warm, too; a rich hazel. "It must have been five years since I last saw you. We were just little bantlings then."

"That's right," said Effie, smiling. "You used to live in the tenement just across the hall. I wondered about you for years. Didn't you say that your family moved to the country?"

"Yes, well." Willie shrugged, his smile fading. "Mama's gone. It was consumption. Papa took to the bottle in the end. I came here for work."

"I'm sorry," said Effie.

"It's all right. It's better than being there with him being up the pole most of the time," said Willie. "I have work at the docks and somewhere to stay, so it's all right. How about you, Effie?" His good humor returned, and he smiled at her. "How is your family?"

Fleetingly, Effie thought about telling him everything. About Mama and Papa being gone and how impossible it was to feed everyone on the few pennies a week that she managed to earn. But while Willie's eyes were kind, his jacket was ragged, and there was a line of stubble on his jaw. He didn't look like he earned much more than she did.

"Oh, everything is fine," said Effie. "Everything is just fine."

The look in Willie's eye said that he didn't believe her, but he didn't ask any questions. "It was nice to see you, Effie," he said.

Effie watched him go. It had been good to see Willie, but when he walked away, she felt as though she'd lost something even more than she already had.

CHAPTER 3

Seeing Willie had been the only bright spot in Effie's day. It was cold and miserable, and no one seemed to want to buy fish.

The fog lifted somewhere in the middle of the morning, but the wind that followed was hardly any better. Effie shivered uncontrollably behind the table, walking up and down in a bid to keep herself warm despite her stiff legs. The fish froze on the table; Effie's fingers stung, then ached, then went completely numb. She tried to keep them tucked in her coat, but it wasn't all that warm in there either. Mrs. Flanders' lips turned blue, and Effie started to worry about the old woman when she grew quieter and quieter.

The day finally ended, and as the sun began to slide down the western sky, the cold seeped deeper and deeper into

Effie's bones. She hurried to pack away the fish, which wasn't easy; they were all stiff and hard as planks thanks to the cold. Her fingers froze to them, making them feel sticky.

"Hurry home, child," Mrs. Flanders wheezed. "You'll catch your death."

It felt like Effie's death would catch her. She felt it following her as she ran home, the blood pounding in her veins, fear of that terrible cold overriding her exhaustion. With every step, she was grateful she'd forbidden John from taking the girls out. And with every step she prayed that he had listened to her. She should have locked them in the tenement. She should never have let them go in the first place. And she should have done something, anything, to keep Mama and Papa from leaving them in this mess...

They weren't home. Effie knew it the moment she stepped into the hallway. The door was closed, but there was a silence in the tenement that cut right down into her gut. She froze in the hall, hearing nothing but the hammer of her heart in her ears.

"John?" she called, closing the front door behind her. Icicles jingled on the eaves. "Sadie?"

There was no reply. Effie didn't run, but she'd never walked so fast in her life. She hurried to the door and yanked it open, and there was nothing inside. No fire, no people, no warmth, and no life. Just the bare little room, a bucket in one corner, a new hole in the wall, the other holes stopped up with newspaper and old rags. They were gone.

Just like Mama and Papa.

Something snapped in Effie's mind. She'd been trying so hard for so long to be strong, to be calm, to be brave, but it had always been for her siblings, and now they were gone. She spun around and bolted down the hallway, screaming at the top of her lungs.

"JOHN! ROSE!" she shrieked, slamming out of the tenement, running out into the street, heedless of the ice that shattered under her threadbare shoes. "ANNIE! WHERE ARE YOU?"

She ran around the block, and they were nowhere to be found. Homeless men with chapped lips stared at her askance, and when she ran screaming down the street, people crossed to the other side of the road. She didn't care. She just had to find them.

"John!" she screamed. "Annie! ANNIE!!"

There was no response. Even her echoes were muffled against the ice and snow surrounding her; the only movement was her own reflection in the icicles that dangled from everything. Tears were streaming down her face, growing icy where they touched her cheeks. The world felt like it had spun right out from under her and she'd never catch up.

"Sadie! Rose!" she screamed. "Where are you? Where are you?"

Nothing. No one. Just the sound of the cold wind. Effie was standing in the middle of the street, but she didn't care. She sagged to the ground, each sob shaking every bone in her body, not caring that the cold mud was soaking into her dress. The world felt utterly desolate. It was almost too much effort to raise her head and look around one last time.

And finally, there they were, coming up the street toward her. John, with Annie on his hip, his arm curled around her; Rose held his free hand, Sadie on the other side of Rose. Effie could see even from this distance how badly Annie was shivering. She leaped to her feet, her tears drying.

"John!" she cried, running toward them. "Oh, girls!" She threw her arms around John and Annie, pulling them both tight to her chest. "Oh, I was so afraid."

"Why are you covered in mud?" asked Rose.

"Where have you been?" Effie cried, pulling back to stare at John.

"We…" John lowered his eyes, and Effie felt a hot coal of anger in her gut.

"Don't tell me…" she began, rage rising in her throat, and then Annie raised her head and Effie saw that the child's lips were as blue as ice. Her breath caught in her throat, and Annie's eyes were beseeching.

"Effie, my hand hurts," she whispered, holding up her right

hand. The skin was a blazing red, mottled with startling white.

"Oh, darling." Effie grabbed the child, yanking her out of John's grip, and cradled her close. "Come. Come on. Let's go get you warmed up."

She jogged back to the tenement, John, Rose, and Sadie hot on her heels, feeling how icy Annie's skin was to the touch. That little hand – it was terrifying to behold. Effie didn't know what was happening to it, but she knew that it couldn't be anything good.

She shoved the front door of the tenement open and stormed inside, clutching Annie. John closed it softly behind them. "Effie…" he began.

"No, John," said Effie. "I don't want to hear it." She kicked open their door. "Start a fire," she snapped. "Sadie, Rose, are you two wet?"

"No, Effie," said Sadie, staring at her with wide eyes. "We're just cold."

"Wrap yourselves in those blankets," said Effie. She knelt down, setting Annie on the mantelpiece, and felt the child's clothes. They weren't wet, but Annie was shivering uncontrollably. Effie pulled off her coat and wrapped it around Annie's shoulders. "John, get the fire!" she yelled.

"I – I'm trying. I'm trying," John panted, clumsily tipping a few bits of coal out of the bucket and into the fireplace. He reached shakily for their battered tinderbox.

"My hand hurts," Annie whimpered. "Why does it look so funny?" She grasped it in her other hand, staring at the strange, mottled skin. "It hurts," she said again, and began to cry, a thin wail that echoed through the tenement.

At least she was crying. The sound sliced through Effie's aching head, but crying was better than being quiet. She looked up at John. "John, where is that fire?" she demanded.

"It's damp, Effie," John exploded. He threw down the tinderbox. "I can't make a fire with damp tinder!"

"Don't shout at me." Effie lunged to her feet, facing John as she folded her arms. "I'm not the one who let the fire go out."

"What would you have me do?" John yelled. "Starve? At least I gave the girls something to eat!"

"What good will that do if they get sick, John?" Effie gestured sharply at Annie. "What use is it? You should have stayed inside. If you had listened to me, then this would never have happened."

Upset by the yelling, Annie began to cry harder. John's eyes filled with tears as he stared down at the child's hand. "I had to do something," he whispered.

His tears startled her out of her anger. She swallowed hard, regretting her rage. "Well, next time you have to listen, John," she said coldly. "Please. Do what you can to start the fire."

She knelt next to Annie and started chafing her frozen arms, listening to John sniffle quietly as he tried to start the fire. And fear and anger boiled in her like poison.

THE NEXT MORNING, ANNIE'S HAND HAD STARTED TURNING black.

It had been a hard night. Once the fire was started, the tenement was only moderately warmer; Effie had dragged one pallet to the hearth so that Annie could sleep right by the flames. The other girls had fallen asleep, exhausted, even before Effie could give them their meager supper of bread and hard cheese. But Annie couldn't sleep. She tossed and turned, crying with the pain in her hand, and Effie had tried everything – tearing the hem of her dress to tie it up in a bandage, warming it, cooling it. Nothing seemed to help, and it had been very late and very dark when Annie had finally fallen asleep.

It was John who woke her, shaking her shoulder gently until she opened her eyes. "John?" she mumbled. It felt like she hadn't slept at all; as if salt had been rubbed into the back of her eyelids.

"I'm sorry, Effie," John murmured. "It's time to go to work." His eyes were filled with pain. "Can't I go in your place?"

"No. Mrs. Flanders doesn't like having boys around the stalls." Effie sat up, and her blanket fell back, revealing Annie's hand where it lay beside her sleeping little face. Her heart jumped into her throat. The skin had gone as black as tar, and when Effie leaned closer, she saw that the area around the black skin had been peppered with blisters. The sight made her stomach feel twisted.

"Oh, Annie," she gasped. The child stirred but didn't wake.

"What's wrong with her, Effie?" John asked, his voice filled with fear.

"I don't know. I don't know," Effie choked past a throat filling with tears. "She needs a doctor."

"How are we supposed to pay for that?" John demanded.

"I don't know, John." Effie swallowed hard, trying to be as calm as she could. "But we have to find someone."

"Effie?" mumbled a sleepy voice behind her. "What's wrong? Who needs a doctor?"

She and John both turned. Sadie was sitting up, her serious brown eyes studying them.

"Don't worry, dear," Effie said. "Go back to sleep." She got up, tucking Annie's blanket back around her.

"But what's going on?" asked Sadie again.

"Shhh." Effie bent down and kissed the top of the child's head. "I don't want you to bother your head about it, darling. Go back to sleep, all right?"

Sadie lay back, her expression still uncertain. "Are we going to be all right, Effie?" she murmured.

Effie stared at the child's skeletal face, and her heart felt like it was going to be wrenched out of her body.

"Yes," she said. "We're going to be just fine."

She knew she was lying even as she spoke.

***

THE DAYS HAD TO BE GROWING LONGER AS JANUARY marched relentlessly toward February, but it felt to Effie as though the winter was only getting darker and colder and angrier as the days wore on. The winter felt like a living thing this year, as if humankind had offended it, and it was taking personal revenge on the world. More than once, the snow fell so deep and thick that the fish market didn't open at all. Effie trekked several miles through the snow only to find that the square was quiet and abandoned.

Those were the days she wasn't paid, but at least then she had more time to go looking for a doctor that was willing to help Annie. It was one of those deeply snowed-in days when the streets were empty that Effie ventured further toward the center of London than she had ever dared before. It had been five days since John had brought the girls home from begging with Annie's wounded hand, and the black area had been spreading ever since. Effie was desperate to find someone who would treat her.

Clutching a rolled-up newspaper in her hands, Effie trudged through the deep snow. The plows had cleared some of the main streets, but the back streets were still untouched, and she knew from experience that a street urchin like her was unwelcome where the ladies and gentlemen liked to walk and drive. She glanced down at the paper in her hands. It was crumpled and greasy and several days old, but she could still just make out the address of the medical practice advertised in the paper. Maybe this time…

The office was at the end of a street filled with shops and businesses. Effie paused outside one of them. It was a milliner's, and there was a beautiful gown displayed in the window, a cheerful thing in bright yellow. She gazed at it for a moment, wondering what it would be like to be able to buy such things and put them on and go to balls or whatever it was that rich people did.

"Oi! You there!" The harsh voice was coming from the front door of the shop. Effie looked up; a liveried footman was waiting beside an elegant coach in front of the door, and he made a shooing motion toward her. "Git!"

Effie knew better than to protest. She tucked her head down and ran for it, heading down the street as fast as her legs could carry her until she reached the doctor's office. It was a small building, but elegant; there was a little brass plaque on the wall beside the front door. DR. JOSEPH CUNNINGHAM, it said.

Effie took a deep breath. This had to work. She stepped forward and gently tapped the knocker against the front door.

It swung open almost immediately, bringing with it a cloud of warmth and delicious smells. Effie looked up in awe at the young woman who stood in the doorway. She wore a beautiful burgundy dress that clung to her smooth curves, and her lips were full and round, looking like they smiled readily. Except they weren't smiling now. When she saw Effie, she pressed them down as thin as a threadbare stocking.

"I don't have alms for you," she said, stepping away. "Now run along."

"No! Please," Effie gasped. She seized the door in desperation. "I don't want any alms."

The young woman hesitated, still glaring down at Effie. "What do you want, then?"

"It's my little sister," Effie begged. "Her hand has gone black and it's falling off. Please, miss, please, ask the doctor to…"

"You should be in a workhouse," snapped the woman. "That's

what workhouses are for." She shoved Effie back with the flat of her hand. "Go away!"

The door slammed as firmly as a coffin lid. Effie stared at it for a few moments, feeling despair seep into her bones like the cold. She couldn't understand why Annie didn't matter to anyone just because she didn't come from a rich family.

THE SMELL OF BOILING VEGETABLES GREETED EFFIE WHEN she walked into the tenement. It was a bland, empty smell, but Effie was so cold and hungry that it smelt delicious to her as she closed the door behind her. Sadie looked up from where she was squatting by the fireplace, prodding the contents of the three-legged pot. "Effie!" she said, her face lighting up. "Did you find a doctor?"

Effie went over and kissed Sadie's forehead. "Not yet, love," she said. "But don't worry. I will."

Sadie's eyes were scared, and Effie smiled as well as she could, hoping that she didn't look as brittle as she felt. Rose came running across the room and wrapped her arms around Effie's knees, and Effie returned the embrace.

"Ouch!" yelped Annie from her sleeping pallet.

"Sorry, Annie," said John, sitting beside her. He glanced up. "Hello, Effie."

"How is it going?" asked Effie, coming over to John, who was painstakingly pulling the makeshift bandage off Annie's hand. When she leaned closer, a terrible smell rose to her senses. It was sickly and thick, and it smelled of death. Her eyes met John's, and they were frank with fear, but he kept his voice steady. "It's a little less sore today," he said, trying to sound optimistic.

"Ugh! Why does my hand smell like that?" said Annie.

"It's probably getting better, darling," said Effie, hoping that this could be true.

When the bandage finally fell away, though, she saw that nothing could have been further from the truth. Annie's hand wasn't better – it was sloughing off. The flesh had been reduced to a tattered, yellowing mess of torn tissue, and when Effie looked closer, she could see the dull glint of bone. Despite her empty stomach, she gagged hard.

"I don't feel very well," said Annie faintly.

"Annie, don't look at it." Effie touched the girl's cheek. "Look up at me while John puts a fresh bandage on."

John's face looked green as he wound a new bandage over the ghastly injury. "What did the doctor say?" he asked.

"He won't see her," said Effie quietly.

"He has to see her," John snapped. "Someone has to see her."

"Well, he won't, John."

"Then he's a fool, and a cruel one at that! Why would he turn away a little girl?" John shook his head. "I hate rich people."

"Don't start with that," snapped Effie. "It's not his fault that we're in this pickle in the first place. It's yours!"

"I was just trying to help!" John yelled.

"Well, you didn't," Effie shouted.

A silence colder than the winter wind wrapped itself around the tenement. Effie glared at John, and her fear turned rage in her chest.

It was Sadie who broke it. "The vegetables are ready," she said in a small voice.

Effie turned away, her heart feeling ripped to pieces. "I'm sorry," she murmured.

"Me, too," said John, and Effie knew that he was. But that didn't make Annie's hand any better.

Only a doctor could do that.

CHAPTER 4

EFFIE TURNED the page of the paper where it lay on the stall front among the fish, scanning the advertisements for doctors. All of them seemed to want terrible amounts of money – more than Effie had ever had in her life. She tried to hold back the despair and turned another page.

Footsteps approached the stall, and Effie startled guiltily, aware that she wasn't doing her work now that Mrs. Flanders had stayed at home with the flu and wasn't there to watch her. She seized a random fish. "Lovely live perch!" she cried. "Only a shilling a pound! Get your beautiful perch here!"

"That's not a perch." Willie appeared out of the bustling, muffled crowd, smiling above his thick gray scarf. "It's a herring, and I very much doubt it's alive."

Effie relaxed, setting the herring back down on the table. "Sorry," she said.

"Bar that," said Willie. "It's all right." He paused. "You look so tired, Effie. What's the matter?"

Effie glanced around. The market was winding down for the afternoon; the buzz of voices and the occasional cries of the vendors had died down, and many people were already packing up their stalls. She looked up at Willie, and the genuine concern in his eyes touched her to the core. "It's..." Her eyes filled with tears, and they clogged her throat, stopping her from speaking.

Willie laid a hand on her shoulder. His hand was steady. "Let me help you pack this away," he said, "and you can tell me everything."

They worked together, and Effie told him everything: about Mama and Papa leaving, about being the only breadwinner in the house, about John trying to help. Every word she said seemed to cut Willie deeper; his eyes never left her, and they grew huge and sad.

"And now Annie's hands are infected," Effie said, closing the lid on the cistern. "I don't know what to do, Willie. I'm so afraid she's going to..." She couldn't finish the sentence.

"I can help," said Willie. He grasped her hand. "Don't worry. I can help you."

"No." Effie gently tugged her hand away. "No, I know you're

not earning much money yourself. They're my family. I'll take care of them."

"I can't help you with money, as much as I would want to," said Willie. "But I can help you to find a doctor to look after Annie."

"I don't know." Effie sighed, sitting down on the edge of the cistern. "I've been to so many doctors over the past few days, and none of them will see her. Most of them won't even speak to me. One set his dogs on me, and I only just got away."

"I know a doctor who's different," said Willie. He touched her shoulder. "He can help."

Effie looked up at him. His eyes were so kind, so brightly hazel, and they stirred something in her gut – something that felt a little like hope. "He can?"

"Yes. When one of the lads cut his hand at the docks, he told me about the doctor," said Willie. "He helps poor people sometimes and doesn't charge anything for it." He dug around in his pocket, producing a battered cloth wallet. "I knew I'd need him someday, and I wrote down his address."

"You can read?" asked Effie, admiringly.

Willie shrugged. "Things were better once," he said simply. "Here." He pulled out a slip of paper. "It's only a few blocks away. Come on – let's get Annie and go."

"Oh, it's so kind of you, Willie," said Effie, her heart hammering, daring to believe that she might really be able to get help for Annie. "It's all right, though. John and I will take her if you'd just give me directions."

"No, no. There's no reason for John and the other girls to come out in this cold," said Willie. "You and I can do it. Come along."

He held out his hand to her, and Effie felt for the first time that she wasn't completely alone in caring for her family. This time, she took his hand. He was only a few years older than she was, but his hand was big and hard and steady, like a man's hand, and it made her want to trust him.

Effie knew Annie was feverish even before she touched the back of her hand to the ailing child's red cheek, as red as her hair, and felt its unnatural heat. "Annie, my darling," she said softly, tucking her wild hair behind her ear. "Wake up."

Annie's eyelids, perfect copper strands, fluttered for a moment before she looked up. She clutched her bandaged hand to her chest, protecting it. "I want to sleep, Effie," she said.

"I know, love, but we're going to take you to the doctor now," said Effie.

Annie nodded in mute agreement and held out her arms. Effie

scooped her up gently, letting her arms settle around her neck. "Stay with the girls, John," she said. "We'll be back soon."

John looked up at Willie, who was head and shoulders taller and about twice as wide. He held out a scrawny hand. "Thank you for helping us, Willie," he said.

Willie clasped his hand in return. "Anytime," he said. "Come on, Effie. Let's go."

Effie held Annie close, feeling the strange heat of her fever, as she followed Willie quietly through the street. He was leading her closer toward central London again, back among the shops full of things that nobody really needed, filled with people who had money to buy something that wasn't essential to survival. This time, Effie didn't think about them. She was too busy worrying about the shallow little breaths of the child in her arms, which huffed warm against her neck. "She's burning up," she whispered.

"It'll be all right. Dr. Snow will help," said Willie.

"Dr. Snow?" Effie shook her head. "His name suits the weather."

Willie smiled. "If what my friend said is true, then it doesn't suit his kindness," he said.

The snow crunched under their feet as Willie led her along the sidewalk toward the servant's entrance of a rambling manor house with a looming facade that seemed to frown down at them as they approached. Effie stayed close, clinging to Annie. They passed an elegant fountain, frozen solid, the ice sparkling in the last of the evening light as if it had been carved of diamond; long lawns were covered in snow now, but there were still elegant trees lining the driveway. Even the path that they took to the servant's entrance was trimmed with neat, squat hedges.

"This house is so big," Effie whispered.

"I've never been in a manor house before," said Willie, looking momentarily daunted. He squared his shoulders. "Don't worry. We'll be all right."

He raised his gloved knuckles and rapped on the narrow door, shaking a bank of snow loose from the lintel. It poured down Effie's back, sending cold trickling under her clothes, and she shuddered.

The door swung open, and a pretty, pale girl about the same age as Effie stood there staring at them. "Cook says we don't have no work, if that's what you want," she said.

Effie's heart sank. This was going to be just like all the other places: a disaster.

"No, no," said Willie. "We... ah... we're here to see Dr. Snow." He touched Annie's arm. "For the little one's hand."

"Dr. Snow? These aren't his offices, you know," snapped the girl.

"So he isn't home?" asked Effie, dismayed.

"He's home, all right, but this ain't exactly where he sees patients."

"Patricia!"

A tall, sturdy middle-aged woman stomped into view, eclipsing the pale Patricia. She swept Effie and Annie with a glance, and her features softened. "Patients for Dr. Snow?" she asked.

Effie's courage had failed her. All she could do was to nod mutely.

"Don't mind Patty. She's got a sharp tongue on her, but her heart's in the right place," said the woman. "I'm Cookie. Here." She reached out, engulfing Effie's arm in a giant, warm hand. "Come along inside and I'll send a boy up to tell Dr. Snow you're here. He's at supper with guests now, but you won't mind a little wait, will you? Not if I sit you by the fire and give you something to eat."

Effie stared at her. "Something to eat?" she croaked.

"Of course," said Cookie. "We won't let guests go hungry."

Effie wasn't sure what was happening to her. She allowed herself to be steered to a bench by the enormous fireplace, which seemed so full of warmth and light that just looking at it warmed her from the inside out. Annie cried out in delight, stretching out her uninjured hand toward the dancing flames.

"Here you go," said Cookie comfortably, planting a tray between Willie and Effie. Effie couldn't believe her eyes. There were three giant bowls of soup, and this wasn't the soup that she knew; instead of watery and colorless, it was thick and creamy, and there were bits of good meat floating in it and fresh vegetables and large floury chunks of potatoes. She seized a spoon and took an enormous mouthful. It was too hot, and it burned all the way down, but it felt wonderful. The taste was unlike anything she'd had before. Willie was gulping it down; even Annie, flushed though her cheeks were, started to sip it tentatively.

Effie was mopping out her bowl with a piece of bread – real, soft, white bread that had been baked that very day – when the kitchen door swung open. To her astonishment, a tall gentleman with coat tails and a top hat and long, curled whiskers stepped inside. He looked distinguished at first glance, but that was before Effie noticed the scars. The entire right side of the doctor's face was waxy and disfigured, the skin looking almost molten, mottled red and yellow. She couldn't help gaping at him.

"Is this our guest, eh?" he barked, so sharply that Annie and Willie both jumped.

"Yes, sir," said Cookie. "You needn't have come so quickly; they can wait until after supper."

The old gentleman studied Effie with very sharp blue eyes,

and she trembled a little. Maybe this had been a bad idea, even if they had gotten a hot meal out of it.

"No," he said. "No, they can't wait. Not this little girl." He strode over to the fireplace in one gigantic stride and crouched down beside Annie. She turned, and Effie waited for her to scream at the sight of the scarred face. Instead, Annie cocked her head, looking at the gentleman with interest. "Your face looks funny," she said.

"And your hand looks funny," said the gentleman, solemnly. "It's too late to fix my face, but perhaps I can have a look at your hand?"

His voice was still stern, but Annie seemed totally unafraid. She held out her bandaged hand, and the doctor touched her cheek.

"She's burning up," he muttered. "Cookie, draw some clean water."

"Yes, sir," said Cookie, apparently unfazed by her sudden promotion to nurse. She bustled off, and the doctor gently touched Annie's neck. "What happened?" he asked.

"She went out in the cold, sir," said Effie. "About six days ago. When she got back, her hand was all red and white."

"Ah, yes," said the doctor sadly. "It'll be frostbite. This winter has been fraught with it."

"I know she shouldn't have been out," cried Effie. "She should have been in the warm, in a house like this, not..." She couldn't finish.

Dr. Snow looked up, and the look in his eye had changed. It wasn't pity exactly, nor compassion, but a kind of sorrow that Effie felt deep in her own gut. For an instant, she felt as though Dr. Snow knew how she felt. As if he'd been there.

"Let's have a look, then," he said quietly.

When he gently peeled back the sticky, damp bandages from Annie's hand, the child gave a gasp of pain and looked away. Effie didn't, but she wished that she had. The smell coming from what used to be Annie's hand was horrifying. The sight was even worse. Her flesh seemed to have melted away from the bones; there were ribbons of ruined skin hanging from the ends of three of her fingers, and a thick yellow ooze pervaded everything. Effie's stomach heaved, but she couldn't draw her eyes away. Beside her, a soft gasp escaped Willie.

The doctor didn't seem to be surprised or revolted. He gave a quiet sigh. "It's as I thought," he said. "Cookie, where's that water?"

"Right here, sir," said Cookie, coming over with a pail of hot water from the fire. "And here's some of your bandages. Patty! Find a parlor-maid and send her up for the master's medicine bag, there's a dear."

Patty turned out to be a dear after all and scurried off, and Effie somehow managed to drag her eyes away as Dr. Snow dipped a soft cloth into the hot water and gently started cleaning Annie's hand. Effie clutched the child's uninjured hand, terrified that she would howl in pain, but she didn't seem to mind at all as Cookie distracted her with sweet treats and stories. "Doesn't it hurt?" she asked.

"Not a bit," said Annie, smiling. "I think it's getting better."

Effie looked up at Dr. Snow, who met her eyes. There was that sorrow again. He gave his head a tiny shake, and her stomach swooped.

It was a relief when Annie's hand had been bound up in clean, white bandages, even though Effie knew what lay beneath those innocent-looking bindings. Dr. Snow gave her a sip of something from a black bottle that smelt of poppy seeds, and then turned to her with a smile that tugged at the disfigured side of his face. "Now, Annie," he said, "you've been such a good girl, I think that Cookie should take you over to the kitchen table and give you a nice sticky bun."

"I'm not awfully hungry," said Annie. She caught Effie's eye. "But thank you, mister doctor."

"Come on, poppet," said Cookie, taking Annie's arm. "I'm sure you'll change your mind when you see my lovely sticky buns."

Cookie led the child away, and Effie tried not to be terrified. How could Annie not be hungry? She hadn't eaten well in weeks.

Dr. Snow touched Effie's shoulder. His hands, for all his harsh appearance and sharp voice, were as soft as a baby's, and his touch was gentle as sunlight. She looked up at him, and his gaze was serious.

"The little one has frostbite," he said, "and the wounds have become infected. I have done all that I can for her."

CHAPTER 5

"Is she going to die?" Effie whispered.

She hadn't dared to even think the words before, but once they flopped out of her, they hung in the air like a fanged, hooded specter.

"Only God knows," said Dr. Snow quietly. "None of us can be sure of that. But you can give her a chance if you take her home and keep her warm, dry and well fed." He paused, and the sorrow in his face deepened. "I cannot help you further. I have given her the only medicine that can do anything for her, and I will send you home with a few days' food. After that, I am sorry, but I have done all that I can. There are so many…"

Effie knew, then, what it was that she'd seen in Dr. Snow's eyes. It was the same thing that she felt every day when she opened the door and looked at her four starving siblings. She didn't have a name for it; it was something that was not quite love and not quite sorrow, but a kind of agonized desperation, a weight that crushed her.

Except Dr. Snow, she thought, didn't have four siblings to care for. This man felt the weight of all London.

"Thank you," she said softly.

"Of course," said Dr. Snow. "Godspeed, little one. Do your best. You will be in my prayers."

It was very dark on the long walk home, and Effie didn't know what to say. Willie carried Annie on his hip, and the little girl fell gradually asleep, her fever seeming broken. Effie hoped that that meant the medicine Dr. Snow had given her had worked. It was good, at least, to see her sleeping peacefully, even though the once-rosy cheeks now looked sickly and yellow in the lamplight that grew increasingly thinner and more rare as they headed closer and closer to Whitechapel.

Effie clutched a canvas bag, feeling the warmth of fresh bread soaking through the rough fabric and onto her skin. At least her little siblings would eat well tonight, but she didn't know where the next night's food would come from, or the next, or the next.

The rising tide of her fear was hovering above her, yet it didn't quite come crashing down, and it felt as though Willie was the only thing holding it back. He walked beside her, filling the silence and darkness in all the cracks of her soul with a quiet, happy chatter about things that didn't matter: the shape of icicles, the sparkle of the lamplight on the snow, the funny little dog that wheezed at them from the entrance of its snug kennel. They were silly things, but they held back the darkness. And Effie wished that he would never have to leave.

He stayed with her all the way into the tenement. Even when she had given the bread to the children and they were all sitting by the fire, John dispensing chunks from the beautiful, fresh, white loaves, he stayed. She and Willie stood together in the doorway and watched. She had tried to offer some of the bread to Willie, but he wouldn't take it. She was too tired and worried to be hungry. It was a strange feeling to not be hungry, and one that didn't bring her much relief.

Willie was watching with a smile as Sadie stuffed a chunk of the soft white bread into her mouth. Effie looked up at him. "Thank you," she said.

He glanced down, surprised. "Oh, of course," he said.

"You didn't have to do that – show me where the doctor lives, and help me carry Annie all that way," said Effie.

"It was the least I could do." Willie shrugged. His expression softened then, and Effie caught a glimpse of worry in his carefree hazel eyes. "Effie, will you be all right?"

Effie wished she could say no. She wanted to burst into tears and tell him that he couldn't leave her here, not with the four little ones, not with everything she had to do. Everything she had to be. She was about to, but if she did, what would stop him from leaving?

The thought brought her up short, draining the feeling from her face and hands. What if Willie did what Mama and Papa had done? She trusted him now, and he seemed so kind. But so had they, once.

The brave smile was dredged up from somewhere deep in her soul, and she wasn't sure that it was convincing, but it was the best one that she had. "We'll be fine, Willie," she said. "Thank you very much."

He hesitated. "Are you sure?"

"Oh, yes," she said.

Effie had never been less sure in her life.

***

Whatever the medicine had done, it didn't last long.

For two days, Effie dared to believe that Annie was getting better. She was less feverish now; though the fever came and went sometimes, she could still eat, and her hand didn't seem as swollen. Effie and John worked together to change the bandages once, and Effie tried to imagine that the flesh wasn't oozing as much. Still, three of Annie's fingers seemed to be gone. She didn't know how to answer John's questions.

He stayed home, caring for Annie, while Effie went to work

for those two days. The bread lasted, she could pay the rent, and there was even a little coal left in the bucket every night for a fire.

Then the third day came.

Effie awoke to Annie's screams. Even though she'd been sleeping deeply, Effie was on her knees in an instant as the child's thin voice sliced through the air. She seized the blanket covering Annie and yanked it back, revealing the small child's writhing body as she tossed and turned on the pallet, her little limbs kicking relentlessly. Another scream tore the air, and Effie seized her by the shoulders, fear lancing through her body.

"Annie!" she cried. "Annie, wake up! Wake up!"

Annie's eyes snapped open. They were brilliantly, electrically blue in her ashen face.

"No!" she shrieked, her voice thin and fluting. "Let me go! Let me go!" Her one good fist pummeled weakly into Effie's wrist; the bandaged hand waved through the air.

Effie struggled to regain control over her voice. "Annie, it's all right," she said, as softly as she could, aware that her voice was shaking. "It's only me. It's your Effie."

Annie stilled, her limbs falling, trembling, to her sides. Her eyes rolled up at Effie, but only focused on her face for a moment before slipping away. "Effie," she mumbled. "My Effie."

"Yes, darling. See? You're all right," said Effie. "It was only a dream."

But it wasn't only a dream. Annie's eyes were closing, and Effie gripped her shoulders, giving the child a shake. "Annie! Wake up, love," she gasped.

Annie gave a tiny sigh, her head lolling to one side. Effie shook her again. "Annie!" she shrieked.

"Effie, what's going on?" John stumbled over to her. "Is she…"

Effie couldn't answer him. She stared down at the motionless child for what felt like forever before the tiny chest stirred and Annie drew a shallow breath into her lungs.

"She's asleep," said Effie.

"Why won't she wake up?" asked Sadie.

Effie looked up at her. The girl's solemn eyes were as deep as graves. "I… I think she's just sleeping really well, Sadie," she said, trying to keep the tremor out of her voice. "It's a good thing. Sleep will make her get better."

"That's good," said Rosie, rubbing her eyes and yawning. "Come on, Sadie. It's cold. Lie back down so that we can sleep."

Sadie reluctantly rejoined her sister on the pallet, and they rolled themselves up in their blanket, clinging to each other. Effie ran her fingertips down Annie's cheek. The child was blazing with heat, and her sleep was restless, if that was what it was; she kept stirring, a frown marring her smooth white brow.

John sat down beside Effie. "It's nearly dawn," he said quietly. "What should I do for her today?"

Effie shook her head. "Nothing," she said. "I can't leave her, John – not like this."

John squared his shoulders. "Then I'm going to the fish market. I'll do your work today."

"Mrs. Flanders won't like it," said Effie.

"I've got to try." John got up, glancing out of the window. "If she won't take me, at least she'll know where you are. And I'll find something else. Even if I have to go down to the factories."

"Please, John, not the factories," said Effie.

"We don't have a choice. We need to eat, and you've got to stay with Annie."

Effie wished she could stop him. She wished she could wrap him up safely somewhere warm, not like this, somewhere like the hearty kitchen of Dr. Snow's house. But she couldn't give that to him; all she could do was to say, "There's a crust of bread in the cupboard," and watch him walk away with the stale crust and pray that he'd come back.

And pray that Annie would come back, too, because whichever dream world the little one had gotten lost in, Effie couldn't rouse her from it.

※

THE DAY WORE ON, SEEMING EVEN LONGER THAN IT HAD always been at the fish market. Effie wished Willie would appear somehow. She tried to keep Annie warm like Dr. Snow had said, but the little girl's skin was so hot she half expected the blanket to catch fire. Rose and Sadie seemed to feel Effie's fear as she worked on Annie. They were subdued, sitting by the fire, not talking or playing games. They just stared into the flicker of the coals as if somehow all the answers lay there.

Answers. Effie wished she could have some of those. With every hour that slipped by, she found herself thinking more and more about what she would do if Mama or Papa was to step back into this tenement where they had left their five children behind. Perhaps she'd scream at them, fly at them with the poker like she'd done one time when a drunken tramp staggered into their tenement by accident. Perhaps she'd grip Papa by the front of his shirt and shriek into his face. "Why did you leave us? Why would you do this to us? Why would you leave your own children behind?"

Or maybe she'd fall into their arms and cry with relief. The day was getting long; the shadows of the street lights outside fell like bars across the road, and Annie still hadn't woken, switching between fever dreams that seemed to take her to a different world and a sleep so deep that Effie had spent hours just watching for her every breath. Effie tried to imagine what it would be like to have Mama here right now, taking over from her, taking the weight from her shoulders, but she couldn't. It almost seemed to her as though the weight would only grow if Mama walked inside, because then she would have to face the most frightening question of all: "What did I do wrong?"

Annie stirred. Effie wondered why John wasn't home yet, touching the child's cheek with a damp cloth. "Come on, darling," she whispered. "You can do it. Wake up. Just wake up."

To her surprise, Annie's eyelids fluttered open. The bright blue eyes studied her a moment, and a faint smile tugged at the corners of her lips. "Effie," she said.

"Annie!" Effie dropped the cloth, framing the little girl's face in her hands. "Oh, Annie, my dear. It's nice to see you awake."

Annie giggled, and Effie felt as though her stomach had suddenly dropped into a bottomless pit. There was something disconnected in the way the child looked at her, as if she wasn't really seeing Effie, but was looking past her into some other place. "You're going to be so happy," she whispered.

"Annie?" Effie cleared her throat, trying her best not to sound scared for Rose and Sadie's sake. "Darling, would you like some soup?"

"You look so lovely." Annie reached up toward Effie's face with her good hand, her small fingers trailing across Effie's chin. "I love weddings."

The words chilled Effie to the bone. "Annie, please," she croaked.

"I love weddings," Annie repeated. Her eyes rolled back in her head, and her hand fell limply to her side. Effie would have shaken her if she hadn't tried that a thousand times today already. "Oh, Annie," she croaked, wrapping her arms around the little girl and scooping her up close to her chest. "Annie, Annie, please, don't do this."

The front door creaked, its broken hinges squealing in protest, and Effie looked up with tears cooling on her face. John stepped inside, and his face turned white.

"Effie?" he managed.

"She's asleep," said Effie, clinging to Annie's skeletal little body. "She – she woke up a little. But now she's asleep." She sniffed hard, trying to hold back the tears; Rose and Sadie were staring at her with terrified eyes. John came over and crouched down next to her, trailing the back of his hand over Annie's cheek.

"Did you find work?" Effie asked.

John shook his mutely. Effie wrapped her free arm around his shoulders and pulled him close. "It's all right, John."

"I'm sorry," he choked out. "It's all my fault."

Effie wanted to tell him that it wasn't. But when she looked down at Annie's sleeping face, at the bandaged hand resting on her protruding ribs, she couldn't quite seem to bring herself to do it.

CHAPTER 6

EFFIE HAD NEVER KNOWN the night to be quite so silent. Even on the many nights when she hadn't been able to sleep, something always seemed to be happening in Whitechapel. There were always drunks singing sea shanties as they stumbled along the streets, or cats fighting on the rooftops, or husbands and wives screaming at each other somewhere. But this night was the coldest, the darkest, and the most silent that Effie had ever known. When she stared out of the last windowpane they had left, the snow lay so thick on the ground outside that it seemed to have sucked everything out of the air – the noise, the warmth, the very life of the city seemed to be trapped and muffled under that frigid white shroud. Even the stars had vanished beneath thick gray clouds that suffocated the city in their hateful grip.

It was so quiet that where Effie sat beside Annie's pallet by the fire, she could hear every faint breath that hissed through the child's lungs. Those breaths were coming quickly now; her cheeks had lost their flushed look, and now they had a gray pallor that frightened Effie to the bottom of her soul. She clutched Annie's hand, willing every new breath out of her, at the same time wishing that those breaths would slow down.

They didn't. Somewhere deep in the night, just when Effie had begun to believe that daybreak would never, ever come, Annie's breaths just stopped. There was no fanfare or struggle; one moment she was breathing, and the next she was not. Effie held her own breath for a second, staring at her, waiting for a movement, a breath, anything. Anything that would show her that the worst had not happened.

"Annie," she whispered. Her voice was a single falling petal of sound in the darkness. She laid a hand on the child's chest and waited. But the only thump she felt was that of her own heart.

Effie wanted to scream. She wanted to explode, or set the world on fire, or lose her mind and run into the snow and just keep on running. But she couldn't wake the children. So she just lowered her head onto Annie's motionless little body and sobbed into it, letting her tears soak into the cheap linen dress, until Annie grew cold and the dark, dark night began to turn palest gray.

"John." Effie gripped the rough cloth of his shirt, shaking him. "Wake up."

The boy mumbled in his sleep, rolling over. Effie wasn't having it. She shook him again, more violently this time. "John!"

John snorted, his eyes opening wide. Their fear grated on Effie's broken heart. "What's happened?" he gasped, sitting up.

"Hush," said Effie. "Don't wake the girls."

John's eyes darted toward the sleeping pallet by the fire, and Effie saw the color seep out of his face. "Annie..." he began.

"Don't wake the girls," Effie repeated. She gripped John's arm, pulling him to his feet. "Annie's gone."

She wasn't sure how the words were coming out of her. She felt as cold and mechanical as the lock on the front door.

John's eyes widened, tears pooling in their soulful depths. "Annie..."

"There's no time for that," said Effie. "We have to get her out of here before the other two wake up."

John blinked. A tear coursed down his cheek, and he brushed it away with the back of his hand. "What are we going to do?" he asked.

"I don't know. I..." Effie swallowed. "We've got to eat. We can't pay for them to take her away."

John walked over to the pallet and knelt down, reaching for Annie's good hand. It hung limply by her side, and he gripped it, absentmindedly running his palm back and forth over the blue fingers as if he could bring the warmth back into it the way he had done a thousand times. "I don't want them to take her away," he said, his voice rough.

"We have to do something," said Effie.

"There's…" John paused, swallowing hard. "There's an open grave at the church not far away. I could… I could take her there."

Effie stared down at Annie's body. It was hard to imagine, now, that that body had ever smiled or laughed or danced with her. She had died with her eyes closed, but Effie knew they'd be empty if she opened them. Annie was gone. This thing lying before her didn't seem to be anything at all but another problem she had to overcome.

"I can't bear to think of her lying in a hole all alone," John whispered. "An open grave would be better anyway."

"It's not Annie, John," said Effie, more sharply than she meant to. "It's just her body. Can you take it there?"

John nodded, sliding his arms underneath the body. He cradled her head against his shoulder as carefully as if she were still alive. "I'll take her," he whispered. "I'll be back before you have to go to work."

"Hurry," said Effie.

John turned and walked out of the tenement, and despite what Effie had just been thinking, she felt a pang of relief that it was John who was taking Annie's body away and not some stranger.

At least John had loved her. Even if Effie knew that Annie's death was all his fault.

Effie washed herself as well as she could in the ice-cold water. She straightened out her hair, ate a tiny bit from the pot of gruel by the fire, and then sat on the pallet that used to belong to Annie and stared at the door.

Rose and Sadie slept. She couldn't bring herself to wake them.

She tried not to think about John's long journey through the frozen morning, heading to the church that he'd mentioned. She knew where it was, and it wasn't a nice church; not one of the tidy, sunny buildings that she liked to see on her way to work. Instead, it was a narrow thing built of bare gray stone, with barred windows and a barren graveyard where the stones jutted out of the earth like teeth. Effie guessed that the open grave would be somewhere at the back of the graveyard among the rocks, where nettles would grow in the summer. She'd walked past one before, and she remembered the great hole in the earth, and the coffins lined up together, and the appalling smell despite the straw that the workers had been burning to try and drive the stench away. It had seemed so strange to her then that some people didn't even deserve enough dirt to have their own grave.

She hoped it didn't smell bad in the grave where John was taking Annie. Not for John's sake, but for the little dead child's, even though she knew that what John was going to bury was nothing but a shell.

Annie was gone, and Effie would never see her again in this life.

And it was all John's fault.

When he finally stepped through the doorway, Effie could see that he had been crying. The tears had washed two clean lines on his grubby cheeks, and there was soil on his hands. Part of her wanted to hug him, but when she thought of Annie's last breath, she couldn't.

"Is it done?" she said simply.

"Yes," John whispered.

"Good." Effie got up. "There's gruel in the pot. Feed yourself and the girls. I'm going to work."

She went to pass him on her way out of the building, and he reached out, gripping her sleeve. "Effie…"

"Let me go, John," she whispered. "Please."

She didn't look into his eyes, but his voice was broken. "I'm sorry," he whispered.

It was too late to apologize, Effie thought. She ripped her sleeve out of his hands. "I'll see you tonight," she said tightly, and walked to work as fast as her legs would carry her.

Mrs. Flanders was tight-lipped when Effie walked into the stall. She couldn't scream because of her voice, but somehow the husky hiss she did manage was infinitely worse.

"Where were you?" she croaked, her watery, bloodshot eyes popping. "What did you think you were doing?"

"John..." Effie began.

"John? If you're talking about that disrespectful little waif of a boy you sent in your place, I don't want to hear it!" Mrs. Flanders wheezed. "The child drove customers away just standing here without even touching my wares."

Effie felt the tears inside her. She wished she could cry them; they boiled and burned around like clouds before a thunderstorm, filling her up so tightly that she couldn't take a single deep breath. If only they could burst out of her, perhaps the tightness in her chest would go away. Yet she felt that if she started crying, she might not stop. She might go on until all of her had drained away into the darkness.

"If you hadn't served me well for the past few years, you little waif, you would be out on your ear!" Mrs. Flanders croaked. "I expect better than this from you. I can't..."

"My sister is dead," said Effie.

She felt her voice slam like dirt on a coffin. Mrs. Flanders stopped in her tracks, staring at Effie with her mouth open for a minute.

"She died last night," said Effie. "I was trying to save her, but I couldn't." It felt like her words were coming from somewhere outside her.

"Oh," said Mrs. Flanders, her voice sounding weak and different.

"I'm sorry about yesterday. Did the fishermen bring cod or haddock this time?" asked Effie.

Mrs. Flanders touched her arm. "I'm sorry, my dear."

"Thank you," said Effie, but she pulled her arm away. It felt like Mrs. Flanders' kindness would pierce her; she had preferred the shouting.

She gripped the fish and began to cry them, holding them up for all to see, feeling once again like them – cold and stiff and dead. Like the fish and like Annie.

She wished Willie would come, but he didn't, even though she thought a few times that she'd glimpsed him in the milling crowd. And after a while, she stopped wishing. Wishing turned out to be as useless as hoping.

Rose and Sadie were sitting by the fire when Effie came into the dismal little room. They were huddled together, clutching a blanket around their shoulders. It was colder than ever, and Effie noticed a fresh draft in the room; when she looked across to the opposite wall, she saw that another brick had gone loose, letting in a chink of streetlight and a knife-thin little breeze.

"Where's John?" she demanded.

Rose looked up. Effie saw that her eyes were red; the child had been crying hard. "Effie, why did Annie die?" she asked.

Effie closed her eyes, the question hitting her in the chest like a battering ram against the gate of her tears. She had to keep them inside, or she'd cry her very soul out onto the floor.

"Because her frostbite was infected," she said stiffly. She came over to the girls and rested a hand on each of their heads, trying her best to be compassionate while she held herself inside.

"But why did she have to get frostbite at all?" Rose insisted. "Oh, Effie, Annie was so funny and pretty and she always sang, and things are so sad without her. Why did she have to die?"

"Hush, Rosie." Sadie put an arm around her little sister – the youngest sister, now, Effie realized with a jolt. "Don't ask such things. We're all sad about Annie."

"Where is John?" Effie repeated.

"Right here." The front door opened, and John stepped inside, holding a brown paper bag in one hand. "I just went out to get some vegetables for soup tonight."

Effie felt something snap inside her when she looked at him. She tried to hold it back, but it was easier to let it out than to risk losing her grip on her tears. "You shouldn't go out, John," she snapped. "Rose and Sadie needed you. You shouldn't have just left them."

"I was just around the corner," John protested.

"We can't be too careful." Effie realized her voice was shaking. "We've got to take care of them."

"Effie, we were fine," said Sadie.

"This time, yes," said Effie sharply. "You've got to take more responsibility, John."

John put down the paper bag. "I see," he said, his voice cold. "Just in case I kill one of them like I killed Annie, right?"

His words seemed to do something to the darkness spilling out of her. Effie paused, feeling it fade away in the face of the pain in his eyes.

"I didn't say that," she said quietly.

"But you were thinking it." John pushed past her, heading to the coal bucket. He took out a piece of coal and put it on the fire; his movement was gentle, but his hands were shaking.

"John..."

John ignored her, moving mechanically as he finished poking the fire. He turned away, still not looking at Effie, and seized the three-legged pot by its handle. "I'm just going to fetch some water," he said. "If you think I can do that without killing one of our sisters."

"John, please," said Effie.

He stopped, looking up at her. There were tears running down his cheeks. "You know, Effie, you don't have to remind me that it was my fault Annie died," he said. "I know it is."

"I didn't..."

John was already walking away, leaving Effie in the middle of the room, feeling like she hadn't lost just one sibling. She'd lost two.

WHEN EFFIE WOKE THE NEXT MORNING, SHE SAW THAT HER feeling had become reality.

She knew almost before she opened her eyes that something was different. Lying still on her pallet, curled tightly around little Rose for comfort, she listened, trying to feel what was wrong. She could hear the gentle breathing of her siblings, missing the soft mumbles Annie had always given in her sleep.

All her siblings sounded a little different; Rose tended to give a tiny snore, Sadie sighed often in her sleep, and John...

John. Effie sat up, her eyes wide. But it was already too late. The pallet beside Sadie was empty, and his shoes were gone from beside the creaky front door. She searched the tenement quickly, but there was no sign of anything unusual.

There was nothing. Even when she ran out into the snow and stood there in the cold with her breath curling in front of her, even when she called him softly, he didn't come, and she didn't know if she wanted him to come. She didn't know what she wanted.

And still the wall she'd built held back her tears.

PART II

CHAPTER 7

Two Years Later

It would have been so much easier if old Miss Coates had just been nice about it. Then again, Effie thought, watching her feet trudge across the gray sidewalk, she doubted that Miss Coates had ever been nice about anything. An angry old maid with a hair chin and a giant black mole on the very end of her nose, Miss Coates had done nothing but yell at Effie whenever she'd come into the drooping little fish and chips shop that huddled on the street corner just outside Whitechapel. The shop had a sort of tired and miserable smell, just like the farriers and bakers and tinkers who stopped in there to pick up a greasy bit of fish and some floppy chips wrapped in an old newspaper. Effie's job was to come in once or twice a week and do all of the jobs that Miss Coates hated, which, on the days she arrived, was practically everything.

The front of her dress was oily now, and she kept trying to wipe it away with her hands as she remembered Miss Coates' words when Effie had finished locking up the shop and then innocently asked if she should return at eight o' clock on Thursday again.

"Don't bother!" Miss Coates had barked. "My good-for-nothing cousin has gotten herself into the family way out in the country, and now they've sent her to live with me. With me, I tell you! Well, she can't just stay for free. She has to get stuck in and work." She'd waved a stubby hand angrily at Effie. "Be off with you. Hopefully she can work harder than you."

Effie had known better than to protest. It wasn't the first piece job she'd lost this year, nor the second, and the feeling of despondency settling around her shoulders like a damp and moldy shawl was a familiar one. She thrust her hands into the holey pockets of her dress, trying to avoid the sharp spring chill that was still in the air. At least the last two winters hadn't been quite as harsh as the one when…

Effie shook her head. Thinking about that winter was no good. It had taken so much from her: Annie, John, even old Mrs. Flanders when the consumption finally got the better of her. And losing Mrs. Flanders had meant losing the only scrap of stability she'd ever been able to bring into Rose's and Sadie's lives.

Now there was nothing. Just the couple of pennies that Effie had in her pocket, and the piece of overcooked fish she'd managed to buy from Miss Coates. That would have to be dinner, and maybe they could eat tomorrow, and as for the rent, Effie didn't know.

The trudge of many feet jerked her from her reverie. Looking up, Effie saw a band of men heading straight toward her. They all wore the same dirty gray uniform that hung off their shoulders like sacks with holes cut in them, and they all shared the same hollow look in their eyes. Some of them seemed to see her, but their eyes only glanced briefly across her face before returning to the ground in front of their feet. The sound of their shoes striking the pavement was an unorganized mass of noise; they weren't marching, not even walking exactly, more just allowing their fate to drag them on toward their destination.

For a frightening moment, Effie thought they were prisoners. She stepped back, wondering if she should flee, until she heard a door clang open across the street. Looking up, she saw the tall gray building towering against a sky almost the same dismal color as the stone from which it had been built. The facade was hidden behind a high brick wall with an iron gate set in a square gateway; a guard slumped there, watching the men shuffle inside.

Effie felt a cold feeling creep down her spine like a lump of ice. This place wasn't a prison, it was a workhouse. Looking at it, Effie wondered if it was worse than a prison.

She wrapped her arms around herself, staring at the building long after the group of men had vanished into its open maw. Those men had just spent the whole day doing backbreaking work, breaking stones or something that felt equally futile. The women, she knew, would have been cooking and cleaning; the children would have sat learning their letters under harsh teachers. At least they'd be learning them, she thought. She couldn't read; Sadie was eleven now, and Rose only a year younger, and neither could they. Perhaps…

The thought chilled her to the bones, yet there was something attractive about it in the same breath. Wouldn't it be easier knowing that the two girls would go to bed every night with something in their bellies?

Dragging herself away from the terrifying thought, Effie turned and headed deeper into Whitechapel, leaving the realm of brick buildings and paved streets behind. Spring had turned the snow into slush, and it squelched under her feet as she headed back to the tenement building. In the last two years, one of the chimneys had collapsed, and someone had stolen the lock from the front door. The last windowpane in Effie's room had been broken. But it was still the closest thing she knew to home.

Stepping into the hallway, Effie could hear the girls chattering together as she headed toward their room. She couldn't make out their words, but their voices sounded merry; a burst of laughter greeted her when she opened the front door.

"Effie!" Rose was the first to spot her. Her brown eyes lit up, and the red hair spun on her shoulders as she turned ran to Effie's arms.

"Hello, darling!" Effie laughed, sweeping the child up onto her hip. Rose's chest was bony in her hands, and it was getting harder to lift her like this. "I'm home."

"Did you bring us fish?" asked Rose hopefully.

"Yes, I did," said Effie. "It's still hot, too. Sadie, get a plate."

Sadie stood on tiptoe to kiss Effie on the cheek, then hurried off to obey. "How was your day, Effie dear?" she asked.

Effie sat down on the pallet slowly, clutching the fish in its piece of newspaper. Rose and Sadie were both staring up at her. Rose's eyes were as merry as ever, but Sadie was watching her with her usual solemnity. Effie knew that Sadie had seen in her face that she'd lost the job the moment she stepped into the door. She looked down at the fish in her hands and realized that they were trembling. How was she going to tell these girls what had happened? That they could be thrown out of their tenement once and for all come Monday, that the streets could be their fate? An image of Annie's rotting hand flitted through her mind.

"Effie?" Rose put her hand on Effie's arm. "Are you all right?"

Effie swallowed hard, plastering her smile back in place. "Quite all right, dear," she said. "Just a little tired, that's all. Here – let's eat this fish up before it gets cold, shall we?"

She tore the fish into three, and Rose gulped hers down in a matter of mouthfuls. When Rose raised her hand, Effie noticed that the sleeve of her dress was only coming three-quarters of the way down. Despite the fact that there never seemed to be enough food for more than one meal a day, Rose was growing faster than Effie could scavenge clothes for her. She felt that pang again and thought of the workhouse. Would it be better?

"That was delicious," said Rose, sucking her fingers noisily. She smiled, resting a small hand on Effie's thigh. "Thank you, Effie."

"Yes," said Sadie, touching Effie's arm. "Thank you."

"Oh, girls." Effie smiled at them. The tears boiled against the gate in her heart again, but she couldn't let them free. Instead, she just opened her arms. "Come here."

They cuddled up against her, their heads on her shoulders, and Effie held them close, pushing the workhouse far out of her mind. Because even though there would be warmth there, and food, and even education, they would all be separated. And there were many things that Effie had done without in her life, but she wasn't sure if she could survive without Rose and Sadie.

CHAPTER 8

THE YOUNGER GIRLS were still sleeping when Effie slipped out of the tenement and onto the streets. She hoped they would sleep late; sometimes then they wouldn't miss their second meal as much, and the wait for her to bring food home for supper would be a little less long.

If she could bring food home tonight at all. Effie paused at the crossroads, not sure which way she could go. Up into London to try her hand at begging again, or down toward the fish market where she'd once worked? Once she'd gotten a whole shilling with begging, but more often than not the rich ladies spat at her and the men hit her with their walking sticks. The docks were a better bet, she hoped. She had tried so many times to find her way back to Dr. Snow's house, but without Willie, it was impossible. Sighing, Effie turned and headed toward Billingsgate.

The familiar cries of the fish market reached her ears even before the sprawling market came into view, covered in stalls with the bright scales of fish flashing in the cool sunlight. Vendors' eyes skipped over Effie as they scanned through the crowd; she knew from experience they were searching for likely buyers, and in her well-patched dress with her dirty hair, she was no buyer. She wandered aimlessly amid the crowd, extending a pleading hand here and there to the wealthier housekeepers she spotted, but they all just glared at her in horror and then darted off with their fish.

Mrs. Flanders' stall had long since been replaced. There was a greasy man with an over-comb standing at the brand-new counter where Effie had once sold the old lady's fish, and he had a shrill, sharp voice that sliced through Effie's ears as he waved a live lobster in the air.

"Lobster! Fresh lobster!" he shouted. "Still alive! Get your beautiful fat lobsters here!"

Effie watched him for a while, hoping vaguely that the lobster might pinch him with its waving claws, but it didn't.

Moving toward the docks, she left the fish market behind and headed down to where the rich folk were stepping off the ships after going to wherever it was that rich folk went with all the money they had left over after buying food and paying the rent. She tried her hand at begging there, but all she got for it was several glares and one crotchety old lady who clouted her in the shins with her cane.

The afternoon was deepening toward twilight, and desperation began to claw at Effie's gut. She had to get back to the girls before nightfall, but how could she go back to them with nothing to give them? Her feet turned her around, started to carry her back toward the fish market, which had gone strange and busy and quiet as the vendors began to pack up their stalls. She tried not to look around, desperate not to hope, and kept her eyes on the ground instead.

She could almost hear the girls already, their cries echoing down the hallway. *Effie! Effie!* They'd be so happy to see her. How could she tell them that she'd failed them again, just as she'd failed John and Annie, just as Mama and Papa had failed them?

"Effie?"

Effie shook her head slightly. The hunger must be going to her head, too; for a moment, the voice had sounded just like Willie's. And she hadn't seen him since the night he'd helped her take Annie to Dr. Snow. Sometimes she wondered if the whole thing – Willie and Dr. Snow and Cookie and their kindness – had all been nothing but a dream.

"Effie!"

A hand touched her shoulder, and Effie spun around, raising her hands, ready to defend herself. There was a young man standing right beside her, so close she could smell the sea air in his clothes, and her heart gave a painful thump in her chest. Young men at the docks had never been a good thing for her.

"Get away!" she screamed, closing her hands into small, bony fists.

"Effie! It's all right." The young man held out his hands. "It's me."

She looked past the shaggy beard clinging to his jaw and into the eyes, and they were the richest hazel, the dancing color that had twirled so many times through her dreams. Effie hesitated, slowly lowering her hands. It couldn't be.

"It's all right," the young man repeated. "I know I look different, but it's me. Willie. Willie Green."

"Willie?" The word curled over Effie's tongue, as insubstantial as a wisp of steam.

"Yes!" Willie took a step nearer, laying his hands tentatively on her shoulders. "It's me."

Effie felt the tears she'd been holding back for so long roil and buffet against the gate holding them. It trembled, and barely held. "Oh, Willie!" she cried. Her hands found his arms, and she clung to them. "Where have you been? It's been..."

"A little more than two years." Willie smiled at her, his soft eyes filled with sorrow. "I found work at last, as a ship's boy. I wanted so much to tell you, but the captain was in a hurry. Their ship's boy had died of the pox, and they needed to leave for India at once. I was with that ship all over the world. This is the first time I've set foot back in London – well, a week ago, in any case. I was hoping I would see you."

There was a strange flicker of something deep in Effie's soul. She couldn't tell if it was relief—maybe, it was. Or maybe it was something else, something deeper and warmer. When two Christmases had come and gone without any sign of Willie Green, she had allowed herself to believe he'd left her just like John and her parents. But none of them had ever come back.

Willie was searching her eyes. There was something a little fearful in his face. "How... how is Annie?" he asked quietly.

Effie smiled at him, surprised to find his kind words made more cracks in the walls holding her tears than any of the hardship she'd suffered ever could. She took a deep breath, getting them back under control. "She... she's gone to a better place," she said.

"I'm sorry, Effie," said Willie.

"Don't be. You did more for me than anyone else ever has," said Effie.

His glance searched her, and she looked away, suddenly ashamed of the dirt matted in her hair and the threadbare folds of her skirt.

"Look," he said. "It's not going to be long before I have to go away again but let me help you."

"H-help me?" Effie stammered.

Willie had let go of her arms and was reaching for the satchel that hung over his shoulder. "I'm sorry, I don't have much," he said. "I barely get my keep as a ship's boy, but look, here." Reaching into the satchel, he pulled out an entire loaf of rough gray rye bread. "Take it."

"The... the whole thing?" Effie wanted to snatch it, to stuff it into her mouth, but she pulled back her hands. "I can't, Willie. It's yours."

"Not anymore." Willie winked. "Because I've just given to you. Here." He reached for her hand, gripping it in hard, calloused fingers that still somehow managed to have a gentle touch. When he pressed the loaf into her hand, she felt that it was still warm.

"There. All yours," he said, letting it go. It wobbled, and she grabbed at it instinctively.

"Willie, thank you," she gasped, staring at it. "Thank..."

She looked up, but he was already gone.

IT TOOK ALL OF EFFIE'S COURAGE NOT TO TOUCH THE precious warm loaf on the way home. She couldn't bring herself to put it into the cloth bag she carried over her shoulder; she was afraid that if she put it out of sight it would disappear, just like she had thought Willie did for more than two years. The smell of the hot crust was almost too much for her to bear, but she bore it, hugging the loaf in her arms as delicately as if it was a baby.

She crashed through the door of the tenement building, shouting. "Sadie! Rose!" she yelled. "You won't believe what I've got!"

Bursting into the room, she saw that Sadie and Rose had already gotten to their feet from their usual place playing quietly by the fire. Sadie's eyes were worried, but when Rose saw the loaf of bread in Effie's arms, she gave a cry of delight.

"Oh, look, Sadie!" she gasped, bounding over to Effie and touching the crust. "A loaf! A whole loaf!"

"And it's fresh as can be," said Effie.

Sadie touched it wonderingly. "Still hot, too. Where did you get it?"

"I'll tell you all about it," said Effie, "but first, let's eat."

"Yes, yes let's!" begged Rose. "Oh, please, break off a piece for me, Effie."

Effie looked at the loaf. Normally whatever she brought home was broken apart and gulped down at once, but it felt like this was something special. "Get our plates," she said. "Let's sit down and eat it like – like a family."

Rose scrambled off to dig in the rickety cupboard, but Sadie laid a hand on Effie's arm. "We are a family," she murmured.

Effie kissed her forehead. "Yes, we are, darling," she said. "Now come on. Let's have dinner."

And as they sat in front of the fire together, eating the warm bread that slipped so soothingly down into their shrunken stomachs, it felt to Effie that Sadie's words were true.

<hr />

When Effie awakened the next day, she'd felt different. Not much warmer than usual, and only a little fuller, but somehow, she felt a little stronger than normal. The pallet she lay on was still hard and unforgiving, her blanket still threadbare; when she stepped out into the foggy spring morning, the world muffled in the grip of gray cloud, the city had still been cold and damp and unfriendly. Yet, for some reason, the coldness and misery didn't seem to penetrate Effie the way it always did. It felt as though she was a little immune today, and she wasn't sure if it was the warmth of the rye bread she felt in her or the warmth of the one who had given it to her.

She almost started back toward the docks, hoping to see him again today, but before she could move her feet, something stopped her. It was a horrible thought, thrown open in front of her like a bear trap. What if she went looking for Willie, and she didn't see him? The idea made her feel cold inside. Willie was a sailor, she realized, the thought as drenching as a wave of muddy puddle water kicked up by a speeding hansom.

He was probably halfway around the world again by now. If she went looking for him, she'd find only heartache.

She wrapped her arms around herself, feeling the thin, rough material of her dress chafe against her shoulders. If she avoided the docks, perhaps she could still imagine that Willie was here in London. The world felt brighter for having him in it. On the other hand, if she went down there looking for him, she might find him – or *she might not*. She didn't think she could face that possibility. Turning around, Effie's feet took her back into London, heading into the place where there were manor homes and people with servants. People who might have work for her.

In the past two years, she'd walked up to many manor houses. At first, she'd been looking for Dr. Snow's house, but without being able to read the street signs, her search had been almost impossible – and entirely fruitless. It was when she started seeing girls like her taking out the house's rubbish or sweeping the kitchens that she began knocking on servants' entrances, looking for work. Two years had yielded nothing, but she knew that if only she could get a job in a manor house, she could be set up for life. She could bring food home to her sisters every single day.

It was nearly an hour's walk from Whitechapel through the streets and shop-lined squares before she reached the first of the manor houses. Walking up the narrow path toward the servants' entrance, she kept a wary eye open. More often than not, these houses had dogs – big, angry dogs with yellow teeth whose masters loved setting them on her. She made it to the door safely, though, and gently tapped on it with her knuckles.

It swung open at once, and a woman with an extremely red nose was already yelling when she opened it. "Jenkins! Finally! I thought you'd..." She stopped short, staring at Effie past her nose. "What's this, then?" she barked.

"Good morning, ma'am," Effie stammered out. "I'm sorry to bother you."

The housekeeper's eyes narrowed. "What do you want?"

"I beg your pardon, ma'am, I'm not begging or stealing," said Effie earnestly. "All I'm looking for is some good honest work, I promise. Truly, ma'am, I'll do anything, anything at all."

The housekeeper hesitated. "Well, the cholera took Mindy," she muttered.

Hope leaped in Effie's heart. "Do you have a place open for me, ma'am?" she stammered.

The housekeeper looked her slowly up and down, and Effie saw her eyes lingering on the dirty mats in her black hair, the smears of mud on her skirt from her long walk across the city. The housekeeper started to shake her head, and Effie stepped forward, utterly desperate. "Oh, please, please, ma'am!" she cried. "Don't turn me away. It's not my fault I look like this. If only I..."

"Be off with you," snapped the housekeeper. "We don't need filthy little street rats in this house."

"Ma'am!" cried Effie, but it was too late. The door slammed in her face, and she heard the housekeeper's footsteps hurrying away.

※

The red-nosed housekeeper had been downright pleasant compared with some of the other people that Effie spoke to through the rest of the day as she wandered from one door to the next. One had shrieked, slapped her and told her to get her "filthy, diseased body" off the property. Several of them didn't even speak to her at all; they just shut the door in her face in the middle of her speech.

Dragging her exhausted body back toward Whitechapel as the chill of the spring evening crept out of the shadows, Effie was beginning to feel like life itself was nothing but a slammed door to her. She had nothing to take home to her sisters, and her feet felt like they'd been turned into lead. The streets were busy as Londoners hurried home from work. Effie started begging almost automatically, fishing out the more kindly-looking people in the crowd, holding out a hand to them as they passed.

"Alms?" she whispered, widening her eyes to make them look deeper. "Alms for the poor?"

The gentleman she'd addressed gave her a disdainful glance and stepped aside. "Go and find work!" he spat. "A grown woman like you, too lazy to work!"

"I'm only fifteen," Effie murmured in protest, but the gentleman had already stormed away.

She let out a sigh and turned away, catching a glimpse of her reflection in a shop window. It was a bakery, and it was busy closing; she could see herself vividly because the blinds had been drawn behind the glass. Begging had been much easier two years ago, but now she could see why the old gentleman had called her a woman. Her thin body had developed new curves in the past few months. She felt like an old, old woman sometimes, and wished that she could be a cute little urchin again – or maybe an old, bent one, someone that people would feel sorry for.

"Oi!" barked a voice behind her. "You. Girl!"

She spun around, expecting to see an irate baker behind her. "I wasn't stealing, sir!" she cried out, panicking. "I – I was just looking into the window."

But the voice didn't come from a baker. Instead, it came from a tall gentleman in a green tailcoat who was just then stepping out of a cab that had stopped in front of the bakery. He had a pocket watch on a gold chain in his hand, and a portly figure with bright pink cheeks under dancing blue eyes.

"I didn't say you were stealing," he said mildly. "In fact, if I saw right, you were looking at yourself in the window as if it were a looking-glass."

Effie felt her cheeks heating, but she didn't know what to say, feeling suddenly silly.

The gentleman took a step nearer to her, and his eyes roamed up and down her body in a way that no one had ever looked at her before. He tucked the watch back into the pocket of his coat. "How old are you, girl?" he barked.

"F-fifteen, sir," Effie managed.

"Good, good. Very good." He raised his chin. "Twirl for me."

"What?" said Effie.

Holding up a finger, the man made a little turning motion in the air. "Twirl," he said.

Effie wasn't sure that she wanted to, but she did, awkwardly on blistered feet. When she faced him again, his face was calculating. "A grubby, skinny little thing, aren't you?" he said. "But you'll do nicely once you've had a bath and some fresh clothes, I think." He cleared his throat. "Do you want a job, girl?"

Effie's heart flipped over. "Oh, yes, please, sir," she begged. "Please, I want a job. I'll do anything."

He took a step nearer, and something strange crossed his face – something dark and stalking. "Anything, eh?" he murmured. He reached up with one of his chubby hands, and Effie could smell his cologne. It was a sticky, thick smell, just like his fingertips when he pressed them against her cheek.

His touch sent a thousand cockroaches scurrying under her skin. She stepped back, and he seized her wrist. "Now, now, don't be spooked, little lady," he cooed. "I'll take good care of you, I will. You'll have a warm room and all the food you can eat – and all the company you could ever want, of course," he added, with a dark chuckle.

The chuckle awoke shadows in Effie's memory. She thought of the women she saw on the docks sometimes, girls dressed much too scantily for the cold, and of the way the sailors looked at them when they disembarked from the ships. The way they took those sailors' hands and led them way, and the hollow darkness in their eyes. She ripped her wrist away. "Get away!" she gasped.

The man didn't seem concerned. He shrugged. "Go and starve, then," he said. "There are plenty of your type in London."

Effie bolted. His laugh followed her down the dark alleys and across the damp streets, and it seemed to cling to her all the way back home to her tenement.

CHAPTER 9

Rose stirred as Effie headed for the door early the next morning. "Effie?" she whispered.

Effie turned. Rose was still snugly tucked into the sleeping pallet by the fire; Sadie, sound asleep, lay with a skinny arm draped over her sister.

"Hush, darling," Effie whispered. "Go back to sleep. I'll be back tonight."

Rose reached out a thin hand to her. Effie crouched down, taking the cold little fingers in her own. "What's the matter?" she asked.

"Nothing," said Rose. She smiled. "I had a lovely dream."

"What did you dream?" asked Effie.

Rose's eyes were closed, her little voice sleepy. "I dreamed that you were happy," she whispered.

Effie's heart felt squeezed. "Oh, but I am happy, darling," she said. "I have you two."

Rose had already fallen back asleep. Effie tucked her small hand back under the blankets and stepped out into the morning.

Yesterday's fog had lifted; a soft rain overnight seemed to have washed the whole world clean, and there was a hint of sunshine trying to break through the thin sheet of clouds overhead. Effie hesitated at the crossroads again, staring longingly toward the manor houses. She should go looking for work again, but the memory of yesterday's frightening gentleman in the green coat made her shudder. She couldn't bring herself to go back there. It was a Wednesday, and she knew the fish market would be busier than ever. Pushing thoughts of Willie out of her head, she headed toward Billingsgate, hoping that the housekeepers buying fish there today would have loose purse-strings – or, even more unlikely, kindly hearts.

She was in luck. The increasing sunshine had brought out a crowd of shoppers moving among the familiar oily scents of the bustling market; the vendors were quieter than normal, so busy dealing with customers that they hardly had any time to cry their wares. Effie had to be careful not to bump into anyone as she made her way to an empty space on a corner beside one of the stalls. It sold pickled fish, and the short man behind the stall front looked harmless enough. Effie was sure she could outrun him if it came to that.

"Alms!" she said softly, holding out a hand. Her voice seemed as insubstantial as a falling feather against the cacophony of the market. "Any alms? Spare a penny for a poor girl? There are two little ones at home to feed. Alms?"

A gentleman with a young lady on his arm – his daughter, judging by the matching shade of their green eyes – gestured toward Effie as they walked past. "You see, Penelope, that is why I caution you to be careful. You don't want to beg on a street corner for your children, with no husband in sight!"

"They're my sisters, sir," said Effie stiffly.

The gentleman snorted. "Ha! A likely story." But the girl looked pitying, tugging her arm out of her father's.

"Oh, Papa, do be a little kinder," she said. Her slim white hand slipped into her purse, and she dropped a shilling into Effie's hand. "Go well, dear," she said.

"Come, Penelope," snapped her father.

Effie tucked the coin into her pocket as quickly as she could, feeling a wave of relief wash over her. At least she could feed the children tonight.

She looked back up into the crowd, and that was when she saw the young man standing just across the road from her, beside the corner of a stall selling shellfish. The moment her eyes lit on him, he glanced away, but she had the feeling he'd been watching her. Looking at him gave her that crawling feeling in her skin again. He had the look of a sailor who'd recently returned; his clothes were still stiff with salt, and there was a week's growth of black stubble on his jaw. When he looked up at her again, his eyes were black, and they glittered with something that frightened Effie more than anything in the world ever had.

She backed away, but this time, he didn't drop his gaze. Instead, he took a step nearer. Effie's courage failed her, and she bolted.

Indignant yells trailed her as she fled through the market, pushing children aside, scrambling over boxes in her way, desperate to flee. She knew he was coming for her; she could hear his heavy footsteps, his harsh breathing, and he was gaining ground. Effie was leaving an open trail of angry people behind her for him to burst through, and hunger was sucking at her muscles, slowing her down. Her heart pounded in her ears, driving her faster. She'd read her fate in the man's black eyes.

Then, suddenly, the crowd was gone, and Effie's feet were slamming on wood with the roar of the sea right beside her. Gray water extended to her left, and with a nasty lurch in her stomach, she realized that in her fear she'd run the wrong way. She'd hoped to head into Whitechapel, or deeper into the fish market. Instead, she'd run onto the docks. And there was no one here to see him catch her.

"Come here!" his breathless voice barked, a cloud of foul-smelling breath curling around her face. She swerved, but he'd already grabbed the back of her dress, yanking her into his arms. They were rough and irreverent when he wrapped them around her body, lifting her off her feet.

"No! Let me go! Let me go!" Effie screamed.

He dragged her roughly between two wooden sheds, slamming her against the wall. "Hold still," he growled.

Effie had no intention of doing as she was told. When the man spun her around to face him, pinning her to the wall with a hand on each of her shoulders, she lashed out in blind terror. Her hand smacked painfully into his cheekbone, but her right foot met something that yielded. He screamed in pain, and his hands were gone. Effie shoved him away from her as hard as he could, hearing him crash into the wall, and bolted.

"Come back here!" he was yelling. Effie knew she couldn't outrun him. She looked around wildly for a hiding place, her filthy hair slapping damply on her cheeks. There! The gangplank was down on one of the docked ships, and its interior was very dark and quiet. She had no other options. Not thinking twice, Effie bolted up the gangplank and threw herself into the stillness of the hold.

It smelt of salt and fish and tobacco. Effie squirmed herself into a gap between two barrels and sat very still, her hand over her nose and mouth to muffle her harsh breathing. She could hear the man's voice outside, but the soft lapping of the ocean against the wooden hold made it impossible to hear what he was saying.

Eventually, the voice faded into the distance, and Effie let out a long breath. Her legs were cramping from crouching behind the barrels. She started to sneak out of her hiding place, and a terrible thought struck her. What if he wasn't gone after all? What if he was lying in wait for her just outside the ship? Her legs were trembling, and she knew she hadn't really hurt him. All she'd done was to make him angry. There was no telling what he'd do to her if she stepped outside and he found her.

The thought was terrifying. Effie ducked back into her shady hiding place, her heart pounding so loudly she feared that she'd be discovered. Perhaps she already was. There were footsteps outside, and to Effie's utter horror, she heard them turn hollow as they struck the wood of the gangplank.

Effie held her breath, cowering in the shadows, as the sound of hobnailed boots came nearer and nearer to her spot. There were two of them now, she realized, and fear rippled through her. The man must have gone to fetch one of his cronies to help him, and now they were going to find her, and they were going to pull her out from behind these barrels and—

The thump came from right in front of her, and it took every effort she had not to scream. It sounded like something large and heavy had just been thrown down on the other side of the barrels. There was a smacking sound, like someone dusting off their hands against each other.

"That's the last of 'em, Ned," growled a voice. It wasn't that of the man who had chased her, but it was nonetheless unpleasant.

"You sure?" answered a thin, reedy, boyish tone. "It felt like we would never be done loading the nets."

"I'm sure," answered the gravelly voice. "Come on. Let's shut her up."

And to Effie's horror, there was a long creak as the gangplank was drawn up, and then with a great slam the hold was shut, sealing her in salty darkness.

She didn't know what to do as the men's feet left the hold. If she rushed forth, would they think she was a thief, or perhaps a stowaway? She didn't know what they would do to her if they found her, and she had a feeling that it wouldn't be pleasant. Perhaps they were just shutting up the ship for the night. Perhaps...

The ship lurched under her, a feeling that made Effie's stomach flip over. There were shouts and stomping feet above her, but here in the hold, there was nothing but darkness, and the rocking of the ship, and rising nausea, and the knowledge that she was being taken out to sea. And every moment took her further and further away from Rose and Sadie.

A burst of laughter jerked Effie from her uneasy slumber with her back pressed up against one of the barrels. She sat up, instantly alert. A trapdoor slammed somewhere above her, and bright daylight poured down into the hold.

How long had she been asleep? It must have been hours; Effie remembered thinking that night must have fallen. She tucked herself deeper into her hiding place among the barrels as the sound of footsteps came down into the hold. She hadn't dared to move since climbing on board the ship, and one of her feet had gone to sleep. It cramped painfully now when she stirred.

The footsteps came closer, but Effie didn't think the sailor had seen her; he was whistling a dirty sea-shanty under his breath. She heard him grip something and drag it away.

Another set of footsteps came down into the hold. Peering over the top of a barrel, Effie just caught a glimpse of a burly, tattooed sailor coming down before her courage failed her and she ducked back into her hiding place.

"Look sharp, Pat!" he said. "The cap'n wants you."

"I'm coming," said Pat pleasantly. "Tell the cap'n to be patient. Besides, he can't just push me around like he does with that scrawny ship's boy."

"At least the boy knows how to work," said the other man. Effie recognized his gravelly voice from yesterday. "Why, you'd take an hour and a half to fetch a net from the hold if we let you."

"I don't see what's the hurry," said Pat. "We'll be out on this sea for two weeks, and the herring are running beautifully; this hold will be full long before we turn for home."

Effie's heart flipped over. *Two weeks?* What were Rose and Sadie going to do without her?

The men headed back out onto the deck, and Effie allowed herself to crumple forward, burying her face in her hands. Two weeks. How would she survive – and how would the two girls survive? She thought of them waking up that morning in the tenement, cold and hungry and alone. Her heart shattered in her chest, scattering bleeding fragments to her very fingertips.

They would think that she had left them, just like John and Mama and Papa.

The thought was too much for her. She curled up on her side and let the sobs take her, not caring who found her.

CHAPTER 10

Effie spent the entire day crying, and sleeping, and crying again. It was as if her body was trying to protect her from it all – from the hunger and thirst, the loneliness and dark, and the terrible, terrible longing for Rose and Sadie. The longing was even worse than the fear, and the fear was bad enough.

And the sickness. Effie was grateful that her stomach was completely empty; for all her heaving, it could offer up nothing to vomit. That didn't make the sick feeling in her gut feel any better. Every tip and lurch of the ship sent a fresh wave of nausea washing over her, leaving her cold and shaking. Her stomach hurt from the effort. Her tongue grew bone dry and kept sticking to the roof of her mouth.

When she awoke on the second day – in daytime, chinks between the wood of the ship allowed in little wisps of light –

her head was pounding. She sat up, clutching it, groaning with sickness as she leaned against the barrels. Her sleep on the harsh wooden floor had left splinters in her left arm, but they were nothing compared to the splitting agony in her head. There was a dry patch in the back of her throat, and it didn't matter how many times she swallowed. It made her want to gag.

She leaned her head against the barrels and stared up at the wooden ceiling of the hold, feeling the ship rock queasily to and fro. Her stomach heaved again, but she tried to ignore it. It wasn't as if she had anything to bring up, anyway. She wondered if Rose and Sadie felt as hungry and thirsty and exhausted as she did.

She wondered if she was going to survive long enough to make it back to them.

The trapdoor opened, letting in a searing burst of light that burned her eyes. She dove back down among the barrels, trembling, as footsteps came stomping down the ladder. Effie didn't dare to look as the sailor came ever closer to her. He was humming, and something about the tune was vaguely familiar, but she was too terrified to really think about it. If he found her... She shuddered. She'd seen the hunger in the eyes of sailors when they returned to London. Starving to death would be a kinder fate.

One of the barrels, some way off from her hiding place, made a scraping noise as it moved across the floor. There was a grunt of effort, and the barrel scraped again. "Oh, come on," huffed a voice.

That voice. She knew it. It wasn't Pat, or the gravel-voiced man, or even the boy who had occasionally come down to the hold yesterday, but she knew the voice. Effie trembled, wondering if thirst had turned her delirious. Surely, it couldn't be.

The voice grunted again, but the barrel didn't shift this time. "Why won't you budge?" the voice muttered, and Effie knew that she wasn't dreaming. It was really him.

It was Willie Green.

She rose slowly, and there he was, pulling and tugging at one of the heavily laden barrels. He wore a white shirt rolled up to the elbows, and his forearms bulged with effort, and his boots were planted sturdily on the wooden floor, and there was no doubt about it. It was Willie, her Willie, and he was here, and he was real.

The wonder of it took her breath away for a long minute, and he turned away. Effie almost screamed, remembering herself just in time. "Willie?"

Willie froze. She saw his hands tremble a little and wondered if he thought he was hearing things. She stepped out from behind the barrel. "Willie, it's me."

"No," Willie whispered under his breath, so softly that Effie could barely hear it. "It can't be. I'm hearing things..." He closed his eyes. "It can't be you," he breathed.

"It is me," said Effie. "Oh, Willie, please help me."

Willie turned around. His hazel eyes were wide, paler than ever in the cool sunlight, and they shone. They were the most beautiful things that Effie had ever seen. She stepped forward again. "Please," she choked out.

"Effie!" Willie rushed over to her, his arms outstretched. It was so glorious to see him that Effie didn't think twice. She staggered forward on legs that felt as wobbly as a newborn colt and fell into his arms. He smelt of sunlight, and salt, and the sea. He was so warm and alive, and she could feel the pounding of his heart against her cheek where she leaned against him.

"Effie, what are you doing here?" Willie took her arms in his hands and gently pushed her back, studying her. His eyes were frightened now. "The captain won't take kindly to having a stowaway."

"I didn't mean to come on board. I didn't even know you'd be here," Effie cried. "There was a man chasing me, and I just ran onto the ship looking for somewhere to hide. I had no idea you were about to cast off."

"I heard a girl scream," said Willie regretfully, "but I was making fast the lifeboats on the other side of the ship and the captain wouldn't let me go and see what was happening. Oh, Effie, I'm so sorry."

"Willie, I'm glad you're here," said Effie.

"And I'm glad to see you, but you're in great danger here," said Willie. His eyes widened. "The men here..." He shook his head. "And if the captain finds out, you'll be arrested – or worse."

Effie thought of the broad expanse of the sea that must be surrounding them, and how easy it would be to disappear in its waters. No one would know. No one except Rose and Sadie would miss her. A shudder crept down her spine.

"Don't worry." Willie put an arm around her shoulders. "I'm going to keep you safe. We'll find you a better hiding place down here, and I'll make sure that no one finds you." His voice had grown resolute now, and when he smiled at her, his eyes danced in their old way. "You'll be safe and sound here with me, Effie. Don't you worry."

"I'm so worried about Rose and Sadie," Effie whispered.

"There's little we can do for them now. But don't be afraid, Effie. Sadie's a brave girl. She'll keep them safe until you get back," said Willie. "Come, now. Here – I'll move these barrels to make a little hidey hole for you. And then as we catch the fish, I'll stow the barrels here so that there's no reason to open them until we're safely docked. You'll be all right."

He was helping her to sit down in a safe little nook as he

spoke, and his hand lingered on her shoulder when she had lowered herself to the floor. His eyes were so soft, and Effie didn't know what to say. She'd never had someone fuss over her like this before.

"You're going to be all right, Effie," he said quietly. "Now let me go and find you something to eat and drink. You must be starving."

"Thank you," Effie choked out.

Willie was already striding away across the hold. And though her longing for her sisters had not abated, for the first time since John had left, Effie realized that she wasn't feeling lonely.

"Effie?"

The sound of Willie's voice had become so familiar that it scooped Effie out of sleep as softly as a mother's arms. She stirred, feeling warm and contented. His hand rested on her shoulder, squeezing gently. "Come on, Effie. It's time to wake up."

It was still quite dark, but the soft light cast by a small lantern illuminated Willie's face where he knelt beside her. Effie blinked up at him. The golden glow lit up his shaggy hair and beard, making him look like he was wearing a halo. His smile was tender.

"There you are," he said softly. "Now sit up. I've brought you some bread and a nice piece of fish for breakfast."

"It's so early," Effie mumbled, sitting up. She took the bread he pressed into her hand and nibbled it. It still felt so strange, even after more than a week, to eat more than once a day; her stomach still felt a little queasy in the early mornings.

"Yes, I know." Willie's rough hand brushed a lock of her hair behind her ear, and he smiled at her. The expression warmed her all the way up from her toes. "But I have good news. We've arrived in London."

The words slapped Effie awake. She sat bolt upright, staring at him. "We have?"

"Yes. We're going up the Thames now – we'll be docking in the next half hour, and as soon as the gangplank can be lowered, I need to slip you off this ship without anyone seeing you."

Effie choked down the fish as quickly as she could. Her heart was hammering, and she wasn't sure if she was afraid or excited. The past week had been strange, and frightening, and she'd spent the entire time feeling sick and missing her siblings yet seeing Willie every day – and having someone else find food for her, someone else caring for her safety – had changed her world. It felt so strange. It felt so wonderful.

And now she had to leave it all behind and run back into the big city alone.

Willie seemed to sense her fear. He held out a tin cup of water. "Will you be all right?" he asked.

Effie took the cup and smiled at him. "I'll be just fine," she said.

Willie's expression softened. "You know you don't have to lie to me," he said softly. "You never have."

Effie looked away, ashamed, but he touched his fingertips to her chin, raising her eyes to his. His touch surprised her, but it filled her with warmth. His eyes were gentle.

"I wish I could stay," he said. "I wish I could help you. But we will be going out to sea again in just a few days."

"It's all right," said Effie. "Thank you, Willie. You've saved my life."

"I wish I could do more," said Willie regretfully.

There was a bump, and the ship ground to a halt, making Effie's stomach churn. Willie's body grew tense, and he looked up. "Come on," he said. "It's time to get you out of here, while they're all distracted with mooring the ship."

He took her hand, clasping it safely in his own as he hurried over to the door of the hold. Swinging it open was no easy task for a single man, and Effie tried to help him. At last, for the first time in days, she glimpsed solid ground. It was the docks, exactly where she'd been when the man had chased her. At this hour in the morning, nothing stirred except for the ship she was on.

"Wait until the waves bring us close enough to the dock," Willie whispered. "Then you must jump, Effie. The gangplank will make too much noise."

Effie stared down into the tossing black sea, and her stomach flipped. The distance was only about three feet from here to the docks, but if she didn't make it, she knew she'd tumble into that frigid water and be crushed or drowned.

"Effie." Willie touched her shoulder. "Look at me."

She looked up. His face was pale in the starlight, but his eyes burned. "You can do this," he said. "And you will be here in my heart, every moment, until we meet again."

She clasped his hand a little tighter, and the words flew out of her unbidden. "I love you."

Willie's eyes widened, but Effie couldn't regret her words. She turned around, and it was as if she could hear Rose and Sadie calling for her. She pulled her hand away from his. The ship rocked closer to the docks, and she gathered all the strength she had and jumped.

Her shoes slammed on the wood, and it was too much for her aching knees. They buckled, pitching her forward onto her face. She rolled with the impact. "Effie!" Willie cried.

"Ooo." Effie tried to bite back the small sound of pain as she scrambled to her feet. There was a sharp, stinging ache in her left knee. She looked back at Willie, and he was busy closing the door, and a stab of panic filled her as she realized that he was going away again. That soon she wouldn't be able to see him again. She started forward, but he gestured to her, stopping her.

"Run!" he mouthed, his eyes wide. "Run!"

Rose and Sadie. She had to get back to them. Even though it felt like tearing herself in half, Effie spun around and bolted back toward Whitechapel as fast as she could sprint.

"ROSE! SADIE! I'M BACK! I'M BACK!"

Effie had been waiting to say those words for days. Even the exhaustion of living in the cramped hold for more than a week couldn't slow her down; she had run all the way to Whitechapel. Ignoring the ache in her legs and the stitch in her side, she plunged up the hallway, shouting at the top of her voice.

"I'm back, my darlings! I'm back here for you!"

She crashed through the door, but the tenement was empty.

Something cold curled in the pit of Effie's stomach as she looked into the still, dark, silent room, as quiet as it was the day that John had brought Annie home with a frostbitten hand. Except this time, it was even quieter. She tried to tell herself that the girls had just gone out to beg or look for work, and that they'd be back soon, but she knew it wasn't the truth. It couldn't be. The floor was bare; even the sleeping pallets were gone. There was nothing but a small pile of cold gray ashes in the hearth. Their meager belongings – the blankets, the bucket, the cups and plates – they were all gone, and a cobweb hung down in the back left corner.

"Sadie?" Effie whispered. There were tears gushing down her cheeks now, and she felt her entire body trembling. "Rose?"

Nothing answered her except a cockroach that scuttled across the floor.

Effie felt she could collapse right where she stood. "No," she whimpered. "No, no." She staggered a step back, her legs wobbling. "They can't be gone," she gasped.

It felt as though the dust and the shadows in the empty tenement were reaching for her, trying to strangle her, and she couldn't stay. She spun around and ran back outside. The tears were pouring freely out of her now, a tidal wave breaking down her walls, ripping a great red hole in her heart as she sobbed and screamed up and down the streets of Whitechapel. She screamed their names until her throat was raw, and then she just screamed.

And Rose and Sadie never came.

PART III

CHAPTER 11

Three Years Later

The sound of the sea was the only constant in Effie's life. She could hear its murmur now as she lay curled up on a pile of rags, trying to persuade herself to get up. The glimmer of cold light behind her eyelids told her that morning had come, yet she didn't know if she wanted to face it. The sea whispered a lullaby to her, dragging her back down toward sleep, and she allowed a swirl of warm dreams to wrap themselves around her. She tumbled down into a different world, one where she was waking up in crisp linen sheets and would rise up and pull open beautiful checkered blue curtains. It was the same daydream that she allowed herself every day. She imagined walking downstairs into a cozy kitchen with a hearth fire burning and china plates all in a neat row in the cabinet. Rose was there – Rose as she imagined she'd be now, thirteen years old, with her cascading red hair curling down her back – standing at the sink. She looked up and laughed as Effie came in but didn't say anything. They never said anything in Effie's dreams – they only laughed.

Sadie was standing by the stove: serious, solemn, a young woman by now, but her eyes danced with mirth as she looked up at Effie. And John sat reading the paper with a fresh growth of beard on his jaw and a cup of tea at his elbow.

There was a knock at the door. Effie smiled at her siblings and crossed the kitchen slowly to open it. It was Willie. His beard was thicker than ever, curling; the top button was open on his shirt, giving her a glimpse of a golden tumble of chest hairs. He smelt wild and wonderful and safe. She let him take her in his arms and kiss her forehead, and something tugged at her skirt.

When she looked down, it was Annie. Her other siblings all looked older, but Annie was still a toddler with wide, innocent eyes and a smile she could lose her heart in.

"I love weddings," she said.

The dream was shattered by the blare of a foghorn. Effie sat up, tense, and looked wildly for an intruder, but there was nothing. Just a ship moving in along the Thames on her left, easily visible through the gap in the alleyway. The dream soaked away, taking her hope with it.

Effie sighed, dragging herself to her feet out of the makeshift home she'd assembled for herself over the past three years. She had never been able to bring herself to go back to the tenement, not after the third or fourth time she'd gone there looking for Rose and Sadie. Besides, the rent hadn't been paid for two weeks; if the landlord had seen her there, he would have thrown her out. Her sisters had left the tenement behind, and so did she, unable to face the silence. Instead she'd found this little nook near the shipping yards. The pile of rags served as a fair enough bed; she'd found some rotten planks to push across the top of the alleyway as a kind of roof, and a pile of rotting driftwood nearby served as a windbreak. It was colder than the tenement, but Effie didn't care. She couldn't move too far away from Whitechapel and Billingsgate. Her sisters had to be around here somewhere, even three years after she'd last set eyes on them.

The foghorn blared again. Effie stretched, feeling out all the kinks in her sore muscles after another cold night on the ground. She ran her fingers through her short hair – lice and mats had forced her to slice it off with a piece of broken glass this summer – and began to walk. The first nip of autumn was in the air, and a wisp of fog hung over the Thames as Effie turned her back to it and headed up toward the fish market and the rest of the city.

"Alms," she mumbled, without enthusiasm, as she stumbled through the bustling market. Bodies brushed up against her, but she felt like a ghost – inaudible, invisible, insubstantial. "Alms for a poor girl."

No one spoke to her. No one ever did. Not since her siblings were gone.

She was truly alone in the world.

She continued through the streets, stumbling along blindly, not really caring which way her feet took her. Her search had been organized at first; she'd gone from one block to another, never searching in the same place twice. But the years had worn away at her method. Now she just walked up and down, her eyes always searching the crowd, holding out a thin hand, mumbling, "Alms?" as she searched for red hair or serious eyes. It felt like trying to find a single piece of gold dust hidden among all the sand of the sea.

She'd left the fish market behind, she realized, and headed into a business district. The streets were lined with little shops: there was a barber, and a blacksmith, and a toy shop. A middle-aged gentleman was coming out of the toy shop. He clutched a stuffed toy cat in both hands, and there was a childlike glee on his face that made Effie want to trust him. She walked over to him cautiously, not looking him in the eye. "Sir?"

"I'm sorry," said the man, tucking the cat under one arm. "I don't have alms for you."

"No, sir. I'm just – I'm looking for someone," said Effie. "Well, two someones. Girls. Little girls."

The man sidled away uncomfortably, his eyes darting across her filthy dress. "I'm sorry," he said again.

"Please, don't go. Just tell me if you've seen them," said Effie. "Rose, she's thirteen, she has long red hair and brown eyes just like mine. And then there's Sadie. She's a little older, and she has very straight black hair and very dark eyes, and she always looks sober as a judge. Oh, please, have you seen them?"

It didn't seem like the man was listening. He backed away. "Sorry," he said, a last time, and then turned and hurried off down the streets, casting a last nervous glance over his shoulder.

Did people think she was crazy? Maybe she was. All Effie knew was that, no matter how many years it took, she had to find them.

DAYS DRAGGED ON. EFFIE DIDN'T COUNT THEM OR KEEP track of them; she occasionally heard church bells and believed it was probably Sunday, but she didn't really know. Each day was the same to her. Search for Rose and Sadie and John. Try to find food. Try not to let anyone grab her, or cut her with knives they made by wrapping bits of string around pieces of broken glass, or steal whatever pennies she managed to beg.

She'd just managed to evade one of the latter – and was keeping her penny safely clutched in one hand as she walked back toward the fish market – when she saw him. He had his back turned to her, but she'd know those broad shoulders and the shaggy blond hair anywhere. Effie froze, staring hard. She hadn't eaten in two days. Could she be imagining things?

She wasn't. He turned and shambled away, and it was Willie's walk, rolling left to right as if his sea-legs were still adjusting to the land.

"Willie!" she gasped, but he'd already turned into the crowd. Effie didn't care how tired her legs were then. She bolted forward, yelling his name. "Willie! Come back! Come back!"

She burst through the crowd, pushing people aside, leaving a trail of angry voices behind her, but for a horrifying moment she thought she'd lost him. Then she saw the shaggy hair again. He was walking away from her, heading toward central London.

"Willie!" she yelled. She broke into a run, not caring about anything. Her bare feet slapped painfully on the cobbles, but she was gaining ground. "Willie!" she screamed, and then she was right beside him, grabbing his arm.

He spun around, and the first thing Effie saw was ice-blue eyes looking down on her. The man had shaggy blond hair, but he wasn't Willie; his face was cleanshaven, the jaw weak, the eyes all wrong. She staggered back a step, feeling as though she'd just been kicked in the gut.

"I'm sorry," she whispered. "I thought you were someone else."

"Stay away from me, filthy little wench." The man yanked his arm out of her grip and strode off briskly, plunging his hands deep into his pockets.

Effie's hand was shaking so hard she could barely hold on to her penny. She gazed around the crowded square, feeling empty and shaken. She knew she'd seen him. This man wasn't Willie, but she'd seen him. She'd lost him in the crowd, but he had been here.

She had to believe that, because she had to believe in something.

THE DREAM WAS THE SAME THAT NIGHT AS IT ALWAYS WAS. The cottage; Rose and Sadie; John reading his newspaper, except this morning he winked at her as she walked toward the knock on the door. When she stepped outside, though, instead of a smiling Willie, there was a skeleton standing there. Ribbons of flesh rotted off its bones as she watched, just like Annie's fingers had wasted away. It reached a hand toward her, and her scream shook her into reality.

She blinked up at the damp planks above her. It was raining, she realized, and there was a thin drip of moisture trickling through a gap in the planks and falling on the rags that covered her chest. She sat up, letting the wet rags peel away. Dawn had just broken. Perhaps she should try to fix that leak and then get a few more hours' sleep, but she was afraid that if she closed her eyes, the skeleton would return. She didn't know whose it was – maybe Annie's, or Willie's, or her own – but it had scared her.

Shuddering, Effie got up and stood in the mouth of the alleyway. The rain had hidden the sea from her view; the Thames was gray and covered in tiny ripples as droplets fell into the fetid water. Nothing moved at this hour, and it made Effie's skin crawl. She felt completely alone. She needed to go somewhere that there would be people, and at this time in the morning, the only place to go would be the docks.

Wrapping her arms around herself, Effie started walking. Rain squelched between her bare toes, for a while, at least; once she'd crossed the shipping yards and headed into the docks, she couldn't feel them anymore. There were men's voices shouting in the distance, and they gave Effie a sense of relief. At least there was someone out there, someone else in the world besides her.

Finding her way through a storeroom and out onto the docks,

Effie saw a hulking ship had just come into the port. It was a massive thing, ten times the size of the fishing boats she usually saw; its sails extended so high above her head that their gray fabric seemed to blend into the clouds. There was an elegant figurehead at the bow – a mermaid, her wooden hair tumbling strategically around her chest, arms thrown wide as she turned her face into the oncoming wind. Her nose had been chipped off by something, and there were barnacles clustered all over her tail.

The voices were coming from a group of men down by the gaping hold. They were busy unloading piles of merchandise from the enormous ship: great barrels of wine, huge wooden boxes of spices, bolts of cloth that gleamed in the sullen light. Effie supposed she should be afraid of them, but after the skeleton in her dreams, they didn't look that frightening anymore. She started to pad down toward them.

It was a bent little man, leaning against a barrel and smoking a pipe as crooked as he was, that spotted her first. "Now there, li'l missy," he muttered, puffing out a blue cloud of foul-smelling smoke. "What's brought a wee thing like you down here?"

"If you please, sir," said Effie, "I'm looking for my brother."

"You'll find more than your brother if you take a step nearer to those men," said the little man. He squinted at his pipe, one eye closed, and gave it an irritable little tamp with his thumb. "They ain't good sorts, miss. I'd clear off if I was you."

Effie glanced back over her shoulder into the empty, rainy shipping yard. She didn't think she had the courage to go back that way alone. "Have you seen my brother?" she pressed. "His name is John – John Wilson. He looks very much like me, but he's a little younger."

"I'm telling you…" the old man began.

"Hey, Roy!" barked a voice a little way off. "Look here what the cat dragged in!"

There was a low chuckle, the kind that made Effie's hair stand on end. She took a step back, and the old man pushed himself off the barrel he was leaning against and gave her a sharp look. "Run," he said sadly.

Effie didn't need to be told twice. She spun around and ran back for her little home, her arms swinging, heart pounding, the pain in her bare feet forgotten as she drove herself back to safety. There was cruel laughter and angry shouting behind her, and it drove her on as surely as a whip, pushing her to her best speed as she raced for safety. If they captured her…

No. She couldn't let herself think about it. She just had to run. Scrambling over barrels, slipping around corners, she fled with animal fear. She was just beginning to think that the voices were fading into the distance when a pair of hands reached out of a dark corner and seized her by the arms.

Effie would have screamed if she'd had the breath. Instead she just grunted and fought, her arms flailing wildly, thoughtless in her desperation to escape. It took her a few moments to realize that her captor was talking to her. "Whoa! Whoa there, miss. I ain't looking to hurt thee now."

The accent was as slow and rounded as the ebb and flow of country hills. Effie hesitated, looking up into the good-natured face of a behemoth of a young man. He had a woolly head of black curls and soulful dark eyes; combined with his enormous shoulders, he looked like a lost bullock wandering the London streets. Another shout echoed through the rain.

"Come," he said. "Hide here."

Effie resisted, but it was no use. His forearms were as thick her thighs. He tugged her into a nook behind some barrels and put a sausage-sized finger to his lips. Running feet slapped past them, and Effie let out a long breath.

"There," he said. "Now them fools are all gone."

"Thank you," said Effie, backing away, still not trusting her hulking rescuer.

He let her go. She was about to run when he said, "Did I hear right? Were you looking for a John Wilson?"

Effie hesitated, staring up at him.

"Aye, you must be," said the young man. "You have his eyes, don't you? You must be his sister, Effie. He spoke of you often."

Effie's heart flipped over. It was the first time in five years that she'd had any evidence that John still existed at all.

"Yes," she croaked, her mouth suddenly bone dry. "Oh, where is he? Please, sir, show me where he is!"

"I wish I could," said the young man. "He's a good man, is your John. But he's somewhere out on the Pacific right now – sailing for India when last I saw him."

"Is he all right, though?" Effie dashed forward, seizing the young man's hands without thinking about it. "Is he hurt?"

"Aye, he's well as a sailor can be," said the young man. "He always talks of how he misses you and how he let you down. There's always something he ain't telling me – a secret about his eyes, like. But he's well, miss."

"Oh, thank you." Effie closed her eyes for a second, squeezing the young man's hands in her own. "Oh, I'm so glad he's all right. Will he be coming home, do you think?"

"I don't know, miss," said the young man. "I'm sorry."

"It's all right," said Effie, relieved. She let her hands fall back to her sides. "I... I don't think I need to see him," she added slowly, surprised at the revelation. "I'm just glad that he's all right."

"Aye, he is," said the young man. He paused. "Miss, I'm just a country boy who fell on hard times and ended up turning to the sea for a living. I'm simple folk, like, but I need to tell you something about John."

"Yes?" said Effie. "What is it?"

"When you see him again..." The big man stepped forward and rested a hand the size of a shovel on her shoulder. "He needs you to forgive him."

Then he turned and disappeared into the rain, for all his bulk, slipping away as silently and suddenly as an angel's vanishing.

CHAPTER 12

EFFIE DIDN'T KNOW how to feel about the news about John. She spent the day wandering the docks, avoiding sailors, taking the scraps of food that some of the kindlier ship's cooks threw at her, imagining around every turn that she was seeing him in the crowds. But unlike with Willie, when she thought she saw him, she didn't know what to do. Part of her wanted to run in that direction, screaming his name; another part wanted to flee. What could she say to him? She could say she had forgiven him for killing their little sister. But had she really?

The thought clogged her mind all day, weighing down her movements, making her feel sluggish and leaden. Yet when she finally gave up and returned to her shelter, sleep wouldn't come. The rain had stopped, and a frigid breeze blew in from the sea, whispering of winter where its cold fingers trailed across her skin. She tucked some more rags around herself and shivered. When she closed her eyes, she saw the skeleton. And when she opened them, she saw only a glimmer of stars through the gaps in the planks. They were very cold and very far away.

She must have dozed off at some point, because it was deep in the night when a sound jerked her from an uneasy sleep. Instantly alert, Effie sat up. Could it just be a stray cat running along the alley wall?

It wasn't. It never was. The sound came again; it was a muffled scream of agony, and then a bone-crunching thump that cut the cry off short. Effie knew she should slip to the mouth of her alley and look to see what was going on, but she also knew that there was absolutely nothing that she could do. Tomorrow there would be a body lying on the cobbles, and she would look the other way and run away as quickly as she could and hope that it would be dragged away before she came home.

She curled up and pulled some rags over her head, as much to blot out the sound as to disappear from view, but the thuds and the muffled yelps went on. There were harsh oaths, sounding breathless, as if the speakers were exhausted by the effort of beating their hapless victim. And then a word – a single word but spoken in a voice that made Effie fly to her feet without thinking.

"Please," it said. *Willie* said.

They were killing Willie right here in front of her alley. Effie didn't hesitate. Something dark switched in her mind, and she seized one of the planks from her roof, yanking it free. Nails gleamed dully in the starlight, and she rushed forward on her bare feet, a wordless battle cry ripping from her throat with a force that scared her. When she burst out of the alley, there were three of them standing around Willie's prone figure on the ground; two had their fists raised, one was landing a kick in Willie's ribs just as she arrived.

There were no words, no coherent feelings in Effie's mind. All that there was, was a red, red rage that had been boiling for many years. It had started simmering when her parents left, and when Annie died, and when Rose and Sadie vanished; everything that life had taken from her had added to the fury, and now it was erupting, spewing out of her as red and rich and hot as blood.

She swung the plank with all of her strength, and the back of it slammed into the nearest man's head, sending him flying over the cobbles. The second man dodged and swung a punch at her; it crunched into her shoulder, but she barely felt it, her screams intensifying as she smacked him right in the face with the plank. He staggered back, and she saw the gleam of a knife as he yanked it out of his clothing.

"Try it!" she was howling now, swinging the plank in a sweeping series of blows. "Try it! I'll kill you! I'll kill you!"

The man hesitated. The one she had struck was groaning on

the ground; the third grabbed his companion's arm. "Come away!" he gasped. "It's not worth it."

She flailed at him with the plank again, and the men turned. Seizing their wounded friend, they took off into the night.

The redness of her rage seemed to seep out of Effie's limbs, leaving the corners of her vision. She stood over Willie, shaking, still clutching the plank. She might have stood there forever, watching them run, if the cold wind hadn't sliced right through her clothes to the very bone.

"Willie," she whispered.

The plank clattered out of her fingers, and she knelt down, straining to see her old friend's face in the starlight. It was little more than a mess of sticky blood; his beard was matted with it, his blond hair stuck down to his forehead. She framed his face with her hands, heedless of the sickly warmth oozing between her fingers. "Willie, darling," she whispered. "Wake up."

He let out a groan, showing white teeth etched in scarlet blood, and a shiver ran through his body. Effie saw that he was wearing only a thin shirt and trousers. The men had taken his clothes, and the night was chill. She had to get him back to her shelter. There was a broken old lantern lying there that still had a few drops of oil in it. It must have fallen from the hands of his attackers; she could see him better in that light if she took it with her.

"You'll be all right, Willie," she panted to him, pulling off her threadbare coat. She slipped it under his head and shoulders, trying her best not to let his head knock down on the cobbles. Tying the arms of the coat under his shoulders, Effie gripped it with both hands. "Come on, now. Let's go home."

Dragging him across the stones to her shelter was easier than Effie had expected. He was heavy, but he was also bleeding, and it left an ugly black smear on the stones behind them. She only had to pause twice for breath. The strain of her efforts made her arms and shoulders begin to shake uncontrollably. Finally, she was sliding him onto her heap of rags. It took two tries to strike her flint and light the lantern, and when she succeeded, its flame was low and sickly. It was still enough to see how badly Willie was hurt. His face was a mess of blood and bruises; there was a great red stain in the side of his shirt, and his clothes were all badly torn.

"Oh, you poor thing," Effie whispered, crouching down beside him. "You poor, poor thing."

She pulled up his shirt and inspected the bloodied gash in his side. It was oozing blood, and she didn't know how bad it was. She didn't know anything, and with a horrible jolt, she realized that this was exactly how she had felt when she faced Annie and her rotting hand. A shiver ran through her, and she felt suddenly as though the cold wind was blowing right through the center of her heart. The last sick person she'd nursed hadn't gotten well again. What would prevent Willie from sharing the same fate?

"Oh, Willie," she choked, her voice thick with tears. She didn't know if she could even stand to try. She laid a hand on his chest, and there was a gentle thump against her palm. *Th-thump. Th-thump. Th-thump.* His heart drove on, strong and steady just as it had done the time she'd fled into his arms, and it gave her strength.

She thought of swinging that plank, slamming it into one of his attackers. "I will fight for you," she whispered, and got to work.

She'd been collecting rainwater in a piece of broken clay pot, and there was just enough of the good, clean water that she was able to wash the worst of the blood away from his wounds. She was relieved to see that they had stopped bleeding, although the skin around them had already started to turn black and purple. His face was the worst. She used the last of the rainwater to rinse some of the cleaner rags and bind up his injuries. It was pitiful, but it was all that she could do. No matter how hard she tried, she couldn't wake him.

The cold water and the cleaning seemed to have made his shivers worse; his skin had broken out into goosebumps. Effie tugged him a little further onto the rags, but it didn't help. His fingers were beginning to turn blue.

"No," she whispered. "No, I'm not going to let that happen to you." She grasped his cold hand and wrapped her fingers around it, chafing it. "Not to you."

He was so cold, and there was only one way she could warm

him. She did what she'd been longing to do ever since that long trip out to sea. She lay down beside him, wrapping one arm around his chest, pillowing her head on his strong, smooth shoulder. Her warmth seeped through her dress, and his shivers slowed, then stopped. She felt his chest heave as he sighed and stirred a little in his sleep, his head lolling toward her so that his chin rested on her forehead.

She closed her eyes tight and pressed her face into the warmth of his neck. It was only moments before she was asleep.

THE GREENGROCER WAS A LEAN, DOUR, WRINKLED MAN who studied his next customer with a shriveled, puckered mouth. It was a smiley young lady with a baby on her hip, and she lifted a perfect red apple from the crates in front of the stall. "Oh, how beautiful!" she said. "It looks so crisp and sweet, too."

"Delicious," said the greengrocer mournfully.

"How much are they?" asked the young lady.

The greengrocer looked down at the sign, and Effie saw her chance. Bursting out from her hiding place behind his cart, she dashed forward, reaching for the nearest vegetables – a pile of carrots. The greengrocer yelled, but her hands had already closed around a bundle of carrots. Their cool, hard shapes slid into her grip, and she bolted for all she was worth.

"Hey!" screamed the lady.

"Stop thief!" yelled the crowd, but Effie was already well away. She dived down the nearest alley and kept running, not slowing down until the salty air of the docks reached her. Letting her rhythm slow to a jog, she glanced over her shoulder. There was no one following her.

Relief was short-lived. She slowed to a walk and looked down at the bright orange of the carrots in her hands; on these gray shipyards, they seemed to have sucked in all the color of their surroundings. A swift pang of guilt knifed through her gut. She'd stolen, something she'd always told Rose and Sadie never to do. But if she couldn't feed Willie, she couldn't save him.

Willie. She'd left him alone for nearly two hours. Jogging again, it took Effie several minutes to reach her alley. Part of her had been hoping he'd be awake when she returned, but he was still lying exactly as she'd left him; covered in rags to keep him hidden, his eyes closed, arms tucked over his chest, chin pointing up at the sky.

"Hello, darling," said Effie softly, slipping into her shelter. She set the carrots down carefully on a clean piece of wood beside the clay pot of water. "I've brought you something to eat." She laid a hand on his cheek. "Now won't you wake up so that I can give it to you?"

Willie didn't stir. Effie sighed, pulling back the rags so that she could peer at his wounds. It had been two days since she'd found him, and she was relieved to see that the wounds, though ugly, didn't have any of the sticky yellow ooze that had come out of Annie's hand when it was infected. When she touched his forehead, its warmth was pleasant instead of blazing.

"You're doing so well," she whispered. "Now won't you wake up for me?"

There was no response. Effie settled down in the rags beside Willie, breaking off the tip of one of the carrots and chewing it. It was sweet and crunchy and fresh and good. It would do him so much good if only he'd wake, but there didn't seem to be much chance of that. Grasping one of his hands, she pulled it into her lap and held it tightly, keeping her eyes on his chest as it rose and fell.

"You're going to be all right," she whispered. "I'm going to keep you safe."

She tried not to think of her four siblings, the siblings to whom she'd made the same promise. She couldn't let Willie down like the rest of them.

He was all she had left.

She fell asleep curled up with her back to him, her

head pillowed on his arm. It was so much warmer this way. Effie had almost forgotten how warm it was to sleep against another living body, although it had its disadvantages; a few times in the previous nights, she'd woken up thinking that she was cuddled up to Rose. It was sweetly sorrowful when she turned over and nestled her head up against the strong shoulders of Willie instead of Rose's soft little body.

Yet even though Willie hadn't said a word to her, she felt as though the loneliness that had been sucking at her soul ever since Mama and Papa left was lifting. He didn't have to say anything. Just being with her made her world feel a little lighter, lifting up that weight that sat on her chest so heavily.

The dreams left her alone tonight. She tumbled down into a deep, deep slumber, which wrapped her in its arms and cradled her close to its bosom and gave her a little peace at last.

It was a soft noise that woke her, or perhaps, less a noise than it was a vibration behind her back. She blinked, her eyelids heavy. Her cheek was pressed up against Willie's arm, and it twitched momentarily. Another groan escaped him.

Effie sat up onto her knees, rolling over to look down at his ruined, bruised face. "Willie?" she breathed. She laid her cold hands on his cheeks. "Willie, can you hear me?"

He groaned again, and Effie grabbed for the clay pot, which was filled with a thin broth she'd made with the carrots over her tiny makeshift fire. She tucked an arm behind his neck and lifted him as well as she could, sliding his shoulders into her lap so that she could lift his head.

"Here," she murmured. He gave another moan, and she pressed the pot to his lips, allowing some of the water to spill over his teeth. "Come on, Willie. Drink."

He swallowed, then coughed, his eyelids fluttering. Effie pulled back his hair from his face and kissed the top of his head. "That's it. You're doing fine."

Willie swallowed again, and then again. His breathing slowed, and Effie managed to coax most of the broth into him. The effort seemed to exhaust him. His head lolled back against her chest. She wiped his mouth and beard clean with a rag and wrapped her arms around his chest. "Hush now, darling," she whispered. "Hush now."

Willie groaned, reaching up with feeble arms. She shifted him gently to the rags, hoping he'd rest, and gripped his hand in hers. "It's all right."

The sound he made had a lilting quality, almost a word. Effie leaned her ear closer to him. "Are you trying to talk to me?" she whispered.

She was almost nose to nose with him when he opened his eyes. One was swollen almost shut, and the other was red and bloodshot, but that didn't stop them from making her heart turn a cartwheel of joy. The warm hazel gazed out at her, and she couldn't help laughing.

"Willie!" she cried, clinging to his hand. "Oh, it's so good to see you awake."

He reached up unsteadily with his free hand; it was bruised, and it trembled, but the touch of his fingertips on her cheek was still soft. "Effie," he croaked.

"Oh, Willie, Willie, my dear," Effie whispered.

His eyes were closing again, and his hand flopped down onto his chest, but his breathing became deep and steady and regular. His voice had made yet another breach in the wall around her tears. She cuddled up next to him, rested her head on his chest, and listened to his heartbeat as she cried.

CHAPTER 13

Cleaning Willie's wounds was always difficult, and it was getting even more so as they began to knit and scab over. Effie didn't know what she should clean away and what she should leave alone. She bathed the wound on his side carefully, dabbing at it with a cleanish rag and some rainwater, wishing – not for the first time – with all her heart for Dr. Snow.

It was the fourth day, and there was still no fever. Effie bit her lip, looking up at Willie's sleeping face as she finished with his wounds. Maybe, just maybe, she could dare to hope. She leaned forward, keeping the bloodied rag well away from him, and pecked him gently on the cheek before turning back to start bandaging his wound.

"That was nice," rumbled a hoarse, tired voice. "Can I have another?"

Effie startled. "Willie," she cried. "You're awake."

He was, and this time, it was for real. His eyes were less swollen, and they danced as he gave her a tired smile. "Hello, Effie," he whispered. "I thought that I dreamed you."

"Well, you didn't," said Effie. "I promise that I'm very much real." She smiled at him, suddenly shy now that he was awake. "Here. Let me give you some broth."

She had to put an arm around his shoulders and help him, but when he was sitting up, he could take the bit of clay pot himself and sip from it. His hands shook when he handed it back. "Thank you," he croaked.

"What happened to you?" Effie asked.

He frowned. "I... was out to sea," he said slowly, seeming to search for the memories. "We went to China for spices and fireworks and things. It was such a long voyage, but it was my first time sailing as first mate, and the pay was all right." He let out a long breath. "We'd come ashore and gone to get supper in the city, and I was walking back to the ship to get my things. That's when three men grabbed me and started pulling at my clothes and... and they took my wallet..." He touched his chest, where his breast pocket should be. "I don't remember anything after that."

"They were beating you," said Effie, putting a hand on his shoulder. "They... they were going to kill you."

He looked up at her. "And then you saved me," he whispered, his eyelids sagging gently shut.

"Willie?" Effie gripped his hand. "No! Willie, darling, keep your eyes open."

But his head was sagging onto his shoulder again, and he'd slid gently back into unconsciousness or sleep—she wasn't sure which. Despair filled Effie's heart, and she realized that she wasn't done saving him yet.

HE SLEPT THROUGH THE NIGHT, AND HE WAS STILL ASLEEP early the next morning when Effie slipped out of her shelter and headed out into the frosty morning. It was crisp and clear, with a pitiless sky as blue and pale as a piece of ice. Effie felt like a little mouse scurrying through the city beneath it.

It was a lucky day for her. She came across an old woman struggling to carry a load of washing from the pump to her little home and seized the basket to help. To her surprise, the woman lived in a comfortable little cottage, and as soon as Effie had put the basket down on the threshold, she presented her with an entire shiny shilling. It was enough for Effie to buy a tin pot of hot gruel from a stall on the corner of the nearest marketplace, and she ran back to her shelter with it before it could get cold.

When she reached the alley, she could hear movement in the

shelter. It stopped her in her tracks. Had someone found Willie? She glanced down at the pot in her hand, and that dark, red thing rose in her chest again. She was willing to bet that if she could drive off attackers with a plank, she could do the same thing with steaming hot gruel.

Creeping into the alley on her tiptoes, she spotted movement. It was Willie. He was on his knees in the shelter, one hand pressed to the wound in his side, a grimace spread across his broad features as he tried to get to his feet.

"Willie!" Effie ran to him, putting down the pot of gruel, and grabbed his arm. "Where were you trying to go?"

"You're back." Willie's voice was thin and pale and relieved. He clung to Effie's arms as she lowered him gently back onto the rags. "I woke up, and you were gone."

"I'm sorry," said Effie. "I just went to find you something to eat. Look – here's some nice, hot gruel." She touched his brow, brushing back his hair, almost without meaning to, the way she'd done a thousand times while he was unconscious.

His eyes lit up when she told him about the food. She dug out the horn spoon she'd found scavenging by the docks one day and rinsed it in the rainwater, then offered him the pot. He dug up a huge spoonful of the grayish gunk and blew on it for a moment before stuffing it into his mouth. Effie was hungry but watching him eat was almost better than eating herself.

"How do you feel?" she asked softly.

"I've been better." Willie smiled. "But I feel like I have my wits about me for the first time." He took another bite. "Thank you for this."

"Think of it as returning a favor," said Effie with a smile.

He returned it, making something flutter deep down in the pit of her stomach. His hands shook as he took another spoonful of the gruel and swallowed painfully. "Do you… live here?" he asked, glancing around the shelter.

Effie blushed, feeling shame heat her to the fingertips. "Yes," she mumbled.

"You shouldn't have to," said Willie. He leaned back against the wall of the alley and laboriously ate another mouthful of the gruel, but it seemed to be almost too much effort for his shaking hands. "Wonderful creature like you. You should have a pretty little cottage."

Effie smiled. "I've often dreamed of having a cottage."

He swallowed, wiped some gruel away from his mouth with the back of his sleeve, and leaned his head back against the wall. His breathing was hard now, and he was clearly exhausted. Effie touched his arm. "Are you all right?"

"Tired," said Willie. He struggled to sit up, moved another spoon to his mouth with trembling hands. "Yes, a little cottage with two stories," he said, "a ground floor with everything, and a loft for our room, with a little square window looking out over a garden."

He seemed to be slipping into sleep again, and Effie watched as his shaking hand almost spilled the next spoonful. She gripped his hand, steadying it, and guided it to his mouth, deciding to play along.

"I've always liked blue checkered curtains," she said. "Especially for my kitchen. And a row of china plates all neatly in a cabinet."

"Yes. That sounds nice," Willie mumbled. His eyes were closed now, and Effie gently took the spoon and the pot for him, thinking he was about to go to sleep. His breathing was deep, and he spoke almost on the very cusp of hearing. "And a cast iron stove with a pot belly," he mumbled, "and a china dog on the mantelpiece."

"That sounds very pretty, dear," said Effie. She touched his shoulder. "Come. Let me help you lie down so that you can rest."

Willie submitted without protest as Effie lowered him to the rags, pulling the largest of them over him as a blanket. She smoothed down his beard and reached for some more rags to tuck them under his head. Her hands were cradling his face when his eyes fluttered open again. "What color tablecloth?" he said.

"What?" Effie stared at him.

"Your tablecloth. For your cottage," said Willie. "What color do you want it to be?"

"Oh, I'm sure I don't know," laughed Effie. "I've never had a tablecloth before."

"But you're going to have one," Willie pressed. "I'm going to get you a beautiful tablecloth. What color do you want?"

He was clearly half asleep, half dreaming, Effie thought. The delirium hadn't quite left him yet. "How about yellow?" she said. "It's so cheerful, and I think it would be beautiful with the blue checkered curtains."

"Yes. Yes, yellow would be good." A smile tugged at the corners of Willie's mouth, and his eyes sparkled up at her even though they were half-closed. "You're going to love it there, Effie. I can't wait to take you to it."

"It sounds very nice," she said.

"It *is* very nice," said Willie. "I'll change the curtains. And I still have to buy a tablecloth and some china, but I will. And you'll love it."

"Hush," said Effie. "Don't try to talk any more now. You're very tired. It's time for you to get some rest."

"No... no. You don't understand," said Willie sleepily. "I already have a cottage. With two stories, and a loft and a little square window, but I haven't dug the garden yet. It's all..." He yawned widely. "It's all briers and nettles now."

"I'm sure it's lovely," said Effie, trying to calm him.

"It's very lovely, and when I'm strong enough, I'm going to

take you there so that you don't have to be in this awful place anymore," said Willie. "I promise."

"Hush," said Effie. She leaned forward, pressing her lips to his forehead, keeping them there for a long minute as if somehow, she could make him feel what she was feeling. He didn't protest; one hand lifted to her hair, and his fingers tangled themselves in the filthy, matted locks.

"Hush now, darling," she whispered. "Sleep."

Willie slept. And Effie sat close to him, his hand tangled securely in hers, and gazed at him until her own eyelids grew heavy.

She wished she had thought to tell him how she felt before he went to sleep: that even though her little shack was wet and drafty and horrid, when he was here with her, it felt like the loveliest cottage in all the wide world.

The next day, she didn't feel the same.

Effie woke up in a puddle of icy water. More specifically, with her feet in a puddle of icy water; it had drenched the hem of her dress, and her toes had gone utterly numb. She sat up with a cry of dismay, yanking her feet back onto the comparatively warm rags.

"Effie?" Willie sat up, his hair mussed, eyes sleepy. "What's wrong?"

"It's all right," said Effie, reaching out a hand to him. She looked up. The rain was coming down in frigid sheets, but she'd done her best to mend the gap in the planks of her makeshift roof, and it seemed to be more or less working. If she wedged herself up into the back of the shelter, she wouldn't get wet. Luckily Willie's rags were still dry, too.

"Oh." He relaxed visibly, smiling at her. "That's a relief. I had a fright when you cried out."

"At least you're d-d-d-dry," Effie said, the end of her sentence swallowed in a shiver that ran from her toes all the way up her neck like a cockroach. Concern filled Willie's eyes.

"Oh – you're frozen," he said. He struggled to sit up, holding out an arm. "Come, sit against the wall here with me, where it's warmer."

Effie willingly slid over to him and cuddled into his arm, tucking her shoulder under his arm and resting her head on his shoulder. He wrapped his arm around her, drawing her snugly against him. "There," he said. She could feel his voice rippling through him where she leaned on his chest. "That's much better, isn't it?"

"Thanks," said Effie, already feeling warmed to her toes – and she had a feeling it didn't have much to do with his body heat. She looked up at him. His beard had been squashed in his sleep, and it gave him an endearingly windblown look. "I'm sorry that you were wounded, but I'm glad you're here with me."

Willie tightened his arm around her shoulders. "I'm glad that I'm here with you, too," he said. "I was going to find you as soon as I'd come ashore, you know. I guess I just found you under different circumstances than I expected."

"You were coming to find me?" Effie echoed, staring up at him.

"Of course. All I've ever wanted was to come and find you," said Willie. His voice was a whisper, and his eyes slid sideways as he spoke, not looking at her.

"But why?" Effie murmured.

He laughed. "Oh, Effie, don't you see?"

"Don't I see what?"

"How brave you are. And how strong," said Willie. "I always admired you, you know. Ever since your parents left, and you started caring for all those little siblings..." He shook his head. "My life was hard enough being alone on the streets without four children to care for."

"I didn't care for them." Shame filled Effie's heart. "I let them down, Willie. I let Annie die."

Willie gave her a squeeze. "You fought tooth and nail for Annie. No one could have done more for her than you did."

"And then John..." Effie shook her head, feeling like she was drowning in her grief.

"John?" Willie raised an eyebrow. "What's happened to John?"

"I don't know." Effie hung her head. "I... well, I blamed him for Annie's death. I tried not to, but he knew I did. And maybe it's true, Willie. He's the one who took Annie out in the cold to go begging after I told him that he could never, ever do that again. That's why she got frostbite."

Willie was very quiet.

"When she died, he took her to bury her in one of those pauper's graves," said Effie, "and when he got back, I don't know. Something snapped in me. I shouted at him, and the next morning he was gone."

"You were grieving," said Willie. "People in grief say terrible things sometimes."

"It wasn't just that," said Effie. "Even now, I don't know if I can forgive him. But I know I want the chance." She looked up at Willie, holding back her tears, slowly building rampart after rampart to hold them in. "I'll never get it, though. I haven't seen John these five years. Last I heard he was on a ship to the New World."

"I did," said Willie softly.

Effie pulled back, startled. "You saw John?"

"I worked with him," said Willie. "Only for one voyage to the Caribbean. He was the ship's boy and I was a sailor."

"When?" asked Effie.

"About a year ago. I tried to look for you when I got back, because John said that he'd lost contact with you." Willie looked around her shelter and shuddered. "I must have passed by this spot a thousand times searching for you, but you were never here."

"I was searching for them," said Effie.

"John said he'd left because he couldn't stand knowing he'd been the reason that Annie died," said Willie. "I told him to come and find you, but he said he wanted to leave his old life and old mistakes in the past. He said you were better off without him. I think he was planning to save up enough money to go and stay in the New World for good and build a new life there."

Effie thought of the New World. She had no idea how far away it was, but it seemed about as far as Heaven, as if John were just as far from her, just as irretrievable, as Annie.

Willie tucked his arm tight around her again, pulling her closer. "He recognized me, though we didn't see each other often on that big ship," he said. "And he told me that he hoped I'd find you, and that if I did find you, he had a message for you."

Effie looked up. "A message?" she said. "What was it?"

Willie smiled, and it warmed her from the inside out. "He wanted me to tell you that he hopes you're happy," he said.

Effie nodded. Somehow, the message felt empty to her. Maybe John had meant it when he'd told Willie, but all the same, she wished he'd said it to her face.

Maybe she did want to see him again after all.

Willie wrapped his other arm around her, too. "And what about Rose and Sadie?" he said. "Where are they?"

"I don't know," Effie admitted. "After I got off the ship, when I went back to the tenement, they were just... gone." She sighed. "I've been searching for them for two years, Willie. It feels like they never existed at all. Like maybe I dreamed them."

"You didn't dream them," said Willie. "You're going to find them someday, Effie. I'll help you. You'll see."

"I hope so," said Effie. "I've searched everywhere I can think of, but no one wants to help me."

Willie pulled her a little bit closer, and she felt his beard tickle her cheek as he pressed his lips to the side of her head. Fireworks erupted across her skin where his kiss touched her.

"I want to help you," he whispered.

When Effie woke the next day, the rain had gone, leaving behind a clinging yellow fog that oozed over the surface of the Thames like pus. Even that couldn't staunch Effie's good mood as she lay on her rags, her head pillowed on her arm, gazing at the still form of Willie where he lay beside her.

They'd spent most of the previous day talking. She couldn't really remember what they'd talked about; they'd seen seagulls swimming on the surface of the river, and ships going past, and she thought perhaps they'd talked about what they would do if they were rich one day. It didn't really seem to matter what they'd been talking about. All that mattered was that Effie had never felt less lonely in her life.

She lay still, watching him sleep. The fog had turned the sunlight pastel pale where it gently caressed the smooth curve of his cheek before it ran down to meet the profuse golden thicket of his beard. His eyes were closed, and where the sun touched his lashes, they were lit up as brilliantly as dust motes. A lock of his shaggy blond hair had fallen over his brow, and Effie reached up to brush it back. He stirred slightly, and a half-smile crossed his features.

He seemed so peaceful that she didn't want to wake him. She still had a little money left from the day she bought the gruel; if she hurried, and if she begged a little, she might be able to buy some slightly stiff fish from the market and get back before he woke. She rolled out of her makeshift bed, tucked the rags back over Willie, and set off for the market.

The queasy fog would have been eerie any other day, but as the sun's rays began to pierce it and paint the world in dancing gold, Effie found herself humming as she walked. She didn't know many songs, but she hummed the snatches of whatever tunes happened to cross her mind. There was a beggar sitting on the corner of the street when she reached the market, playing the pipes. If Effie hadn't been starving herself, she would have given him something; as it was, she picked up the tune and kept it in the back of her throat like a sweet flavor, humming it as she walked.

The old man who sold slightly questionable cooked fish in the back corner of the market was busy scrubbing the wooden table of his stall when Effie reached him. She tried not to look at the greenish hue of the water as it was scrubbed off and slopped into a nearby bucket.

"Good morning," she said cheerfully.

He glared at her from among the sullen folds of his face. "Buying or begging?" he grumbled.

"Buying," said Effie, "if you have something for…" She dug in her pocket. "Tuppence?"

The old man sighed and looked down into the pan that spat and sizzled on the fire behind him. Even though Effie knew he bought up all the rotten fish from the vendors at the end of the day, the scent of the oil frying still made her mouth water. "Dropped one in the fire yesterday," he said reluctantly. "You can have it if you like."

Effie put the tuppence on the table and took the fish. The piper was playing a slightly happier tune when she passed him; she found herself walking briskly, smiling at strangers as she hummed along. The whole world seemed like a brighter place today. It was as if she'd been living in black and white until Willie had appeared by her side, and that had changed everything. He had brought color into her world.

The long walk back to the alley couldn't diminish the feeling, and she was practically skipping when she reached it, the fish still good and warm in its newspaper under her arm. "Willie, dear!" she called out, hoping to wake him with the smell of food. "I've got..."

Her voice died on her lips. She trembled where she stood, staring at the shelter, the shelter where she'd left all her happiness behind just a few minutes ago.

The *empty shelter*.

She couldn't bring herself to call out his name. She knew it would echo from one rickety wall to the other, and it would bounce back to her in mockery, just as her voice had done when she'd called and called for Rose and Sadie. Her heart was hammering in every cell of her body as she threw down the fish and ran to the shelter. He wasn't there. Out of the alley. Down to the docks. Along the banks of the river. Staring down into the filthy water. She couldn't bring herself to scream and cry; all she did was run, and search, not caring where her feet took her as long as she might find Willie there.

But no matter where she ran, she couldn't escape the feeling that drummed quietly at the back of her mind, the feeling that grew insistently louder and louder even as the rest of the world turned gray and faraway and muffled. The feeling that told her she'd done this before. She'd searched like this before. And every single time, she'd come up empty.

Every single time she had ended up alone yet again.

※

She did not return to the shelter. It had become like the tenement: a place she couldn't face without the people who had been there with her. Instead she kept on searching, working in circles around the docks, her voice paralyzed with fear, until her legs could no longer carry her. She collapsed in the middle of one of the docks out in the open. It was a terrible place to be, especially as she could feel the world getting colder by the minute, with the fog rolling in so thick she could barely see the Thames in front of her. But her legs couldn't carry her anymore.

She sat there for a long time, just staring into the fog. It seemed to have penetrated her very soul: thick and sickly and clinging. Suffocating. She could almost feel it filling her nose, her throat, her lungs. Squeezing the life out of her with the knowledge that she would always be alone.

She wished the tears would come and wash it all away, but they were locked so tightly behind those walls that she began to wonder if they were even there anymore. And somehow that was far more frightening than feeling their unrelenting pressure trying to burst out into the open.

Effie sat there until the darkness folded her in its wings, and she fell into something more like death than sleep.

CHAPTER 14

SKELETONS. The cottage was filled with skeletons. The skeleton of Rose was setting the table, and it had long red hair, but its face was just a rotten mass with empty eye sockets that crawled with maggots; Sadie's skeleton was just bones and darkness as it turned to take a pretty china cup out of the cabinet. As Effie watched, John's skeleton turned a page on its newspaper. She ran for the door, but when she pulled it open, Willie was standing in front of her in flesh and blood. She cried out, reaching for him, but when she touched him, his bones clattered to the floor with a terrible sound.

The sound. Effie jerked awake, sitting up. The sound had been real. There it came again: the tumble of something hard and noisy falling to the ground. She looked around, but in the fog, the darkness of the night was absolute.

What did it matter anyway? Effie pulled her knees to her chest, feeling every muscle in her body ache with stiffness and cold. She was alone. The walls of her tears trembled, but they didn't come down.

She heard it again. This time it sounded like wooden poles being thrown onto the ground – offloaded from a ship perhaps. Her suspicions were confirmed when she heard the voices just on the other side of the docks.

"All done, boys," the first one barked. It was as rough and snarling as choppy sea in a thunderstorm. "Go off and have yourselves some fun now."

"Aye aye, cap'n!" jeered a mocking voice.

Effie knew exactly what kind of fun those men would plan on having. She scrambled to her feet, but it was already too late. They were coming around the load of timber they'd just taken off their ship and they had a lantern and the light of it was cast in a circle around her, blinding her.

"Well!" barked one voice. "Look at this little beauty!"

The voice had everything in it that Effie most feared. She couldn't see, but she didn't have to. As long as she fled away from the lantern light, nothing could be worse than being caught by those men. She fled as fast as she could lay foot to the ground, disoriented, desperate, panicking. They were laughing as they chased her, the lantern light swinging all around her, throwing images of their shadows every time it swung behind her: she could see her own slim shadow fleeing, but she couldn't count the men. There seemed to be thousands of them right behind her, their limbs flying across the cobbles, entangling with her shadow, bringing it down. There were so many.

She heard footsteps slap right behind her and swerved hard to the right, missing the hand that reached out to grab her so narrowly that she felt the arm knock against her shoulder as she dodged. There was a thump behind her and the crash of bodies falling over one another. Maybe she was going to outrun them. Perhaps she would see daybreak after all -

The ground dropped away from beneath her feet so suddenly that she didn't have time to scream. She flailed once, feeling nothing but cold air around her, and then the impact struck her. It felt like falling onto cold stone, except she couldn't sink into stone. Stone couldn't close over her head and drive her under and fill her nostrils with something that felt like fire when she tried to take a breath. She tried to scream, but it filled her mouth and gonged in her ears, soaking ice cold into her shabby dress, and no matter which way she struck she knew she was sinking. She was sinking in water. She was sinking in the Thames. She was drowning.

She paddled madly in all directions with her limbs, turning and twisting, but everywhere was darkness and everything was cold. Cramps stiffened her legs, and pain shot through her frozen fingers. Her lungs felt like they'd been filled with molten tar, and her head was spinning, and she was spinning, and everything was going numb.

The world began to slip away from her. She couldn't find it in her to strike out anymore now; she just let the water wrap itself around her. It was quite gentle now that she was lying still. Perhaps she was sinking even further. She didn't know, or, truthfully, even care. It felt better to just rest. The world seemed to be getting further and further away, and perhaps that wasn't such a bad thing…

Tugging. Something was tugging at her, gripping her arm. She didn't know which way it was taking her, but it was uncomfortable. She wanted to squirm and pull her arm away, but she didn't have the strength, so she just let it take her. It was pulling, and pulling, and then her face was cold, so cold. It all seemed like too much effort. She reached for that welcome darkness again, where she could just rest.

"No. No! Effie, my love. Effie, open your eyes!"

Why would she want to open her eyes? She'd worked so hard and struggled so much. She just wanted to sleep. The darkness reached for her, its embrace warm and simple. It didn't ask difficult questions. She could be with Annie…

"Effie!"

Something about the voice, though. It tugged at her more insistently than the thing on her arm had, pulling at her soul. She tried to move, and paralyzing pain shot through her head.

But she wanted to move for that voice. She wanted to face the pain for that voice.

"Effie, please!" It was crying now. Pleading. "Breathe for me."

She wanted to. She had to. The red thing rose in her, the dark, scarlet thing that had woken her like a sleeping lioness when the thieves were beating Willie. *Willie*. It was him. Breathe, he was saying. She had to breathe. She would do anything for him – even take a breath. She tried, but her throat seemed to be filled with something, and her consciousness was slipping away no matter how hard she tried.

He pounded on her back, and she felt water gurgle into her throat, choking her, as she vomited it out.

"Effie," he gasped. Then his lips found hers, and a burst of air filled her lungs, setting every cell in her body afire. Her eyes snapped open, and the world was a confusion of lantern light on water. "Yes!" cried Willie. He was clinging to her, arms around her, holding him close to her body. "Yes, my love, you can do this! Breathe!"

Her chest burned, but Effie tried, and a tiny sip of air made it into her lungs. There was water everywhere – even inside her. She coughed, and a burst of it gushed down her chin and the front of her dress.

"Yes. Yes! Again, my love. Again!" Willie cried. His face was very pale right in front of her and shiny with water. "Again!"

Again. This time the breath was just a little bigger, and she took another, then another. Her limbs found some strength, and she grasped at his shirt, clinging to it with all her might.

"Yes! Oh, Effie, that's it." Willie let go of her with one arm and began to swim, propelling them both through the water. "Come on, now. Keep breathing. Just hold on to me and keep on breathing."

Keep breathing. It was all he expected of her, and as she clung to him, it was almost more than she could do. But she kept breathing. One breath at a time, hanging on to him with all her might.

※

WHEN THEY FINALLY REACHED THE DOCKS, WILLIE HAD TO hold onto Effie's arm as he dragged himself out of the water first, then reached down and lifted her by one arm and a fistful of her dress. It wasn't graceful, but when he had pulled her out and rolled her over onto her back, she had never been more grateful for the feeling of solid ground under her.

"Just lie still. Just rest there." Willie's voice was shaking. The lantern light came nearer, and Effie felt something warm and dry being pulled over her. "Are you hurt?"

"N-n-no," Effie managed between chattering teeth. She stared up at his hazel eyes, still warm despite the frigid night. "You came back."

"Of course, I came back, my love," said Willie. "What else

would I do – leave you behind?" He rested a warm hand on her cheek. "I meant to be back this evening already, but when I got to the shelter I couldn't find you."

She was shivering violently. "I was looking for you."

"I'm sorry," said Willie. "I... I left you a note. I realize now that it was a foolish thing to do, but this morning was the first time I woke up able to walk, and I was just so excited to get everything ready for you..." He sighed. "I'm sorry, Effie."

"None of it m-m-m-matters," she managed through chattering teeth. "You're h-h-here now." She meant it.

"And you're frozen," said Willie practically. "Come, darling. There's a boarding house nearby of good repute – I've stayed there before a few times when we came ashore for only a few nights. We'll sleep there, and I'll show you my cottage in the morning."

He wrapped the coat snugly around her, then slid his arms under her and lifted her as easily as if she weighed no more than a bird. Her head slumped against his shoulder.

"Your c-c-cottage?" she whispered. "It's real?"

"Of course, it's real," he said, shivering himself. He kissed her forehead. "Just hold on a few more minutes for me and you'll be snug in a room at an inn, getting all your needs tended to. You won't be cold much longer, Effie. Everything is going to be all right."

Effie closed her eyes. The world had become so strange, but none of it mattered now. "Everything is already all right," she whispered. "I'm here with you."

※

Afterwards, Effie could never remember much more from that night. She thought she must have fainted while Willie was carrying her to the boarding house, because the next thing she remembered was a female voice saying, "Oh! The poor thing! Look at her!" and Willie's voice, "Mrs. Dunn, I know she may look a little ragamuffin right now, but to me she is more than a princess. Please… take care of her."

Then she was lying on something extremely soft – the softest thing she'd ever felt under her tired bones – and her wet dress was being peeled away and the female voice was saying, "Don't you be worrying now, my sweet. You'll be right."

Someone lifted her up a little, and a thin liquid was poured down her throat that burned all the way down but warmed her almost as much as Willie's eyes. And everything was so warm and dry and safe that Effie finally allowed herself to drift away into sleep.

She woke in a small, clean room, with no holes in the walls and an intact windowpane looking out over a bustling gray street. There were sheets and blankets tucked around her; their weight was strange, yet delicious. She lay on her back, and her head was turned a little to her left, where a fire was crackling in the hearth against the wall. Everything hurt, but it didn't seem to matter here in this downy paradise of warmth and softness.

A hand squeezed on her own. "Effie?"

She turned her head. It was Willie, sitting right beside her, only he looked very different than the last time she'd seen him. He wore a coat with no holes in it, and his hair had been cut, his beard neatly trimmed around his square jaw. It lifted when he smiled.

"You're awake," he murmured, reaching up with the back of his hand to brush her hair out of her face.

"Willie?" Effie swallowed; her throat still burned. "Where are we?"

"In a boarding house, my love," said Willie. "But only until you are strong enough to take a ride in a hansom cab. Then we'll be at my cottage where you'll be safe and warm."

"A cab?" She blinked. "A boarding house? How can you afford all this?"

"I've been saving money my whole life," said Willie, "ever since I first went out to sea. The cottage isn't mine yet, but Dr. Snow has been kind as ever – he's my landlord, you know – and after my next voyage I'll be able to buy it. You'll be safe there if..." He paused, his cheeks flushing. "If you want."

She closed her hand over his. "Oh, Willie," she whispered.

"Only if you want," he said hastily.

"Of course, I want," she said.

He raised the back of her hand to his lips and kissed it. "I... I'd like to ask you if there's anything else you would want," he said. "I don't have a ring yet, but I nearly lost you last night, and there's just – there's no time to lose, and..."

"And?" said Effie, a wild hope turning over and over in her heart. How strange the world had become, but how beautiful. She wasn't sure that it wasn't a dream, but if it was, she was going to go on dreaming it for as long as she could.

Willie took a deep breath.

"Do you want to marry me?" he asked.

And really, there was no question about what Effie was going to answer.

"It's not much," Willie said nervously, clinging to Effie's hand as the hansom rattled through the streets, "but I think – well, I think it could be quite cozy."

Effie didn't reply. She was too busy staring out of the windows as they bumped along a narrow little street on a hill, where trees had been planted in the sidewalks. There were gardens here. She saw a dog; not one of the big, angry guard dogs that had chased her so often, but a scruffy, amiable little thing, running around with a group of children in the street. The children had clean hair and shoes.

"Effie?" Willie squeezed her hand.

"Oh – yes!" She beamed at him. "It's all so perfect, Willie. It's all so wonderful!"

His face lit up. "I hope you'll think that the cottage is all right, too," he said.

She slid a little nearer to him and rested her head on his shoulder. "I thought even the shelter was perfect," she whispered, "as long as you were there."

The cab came to a halt, and Willie held the door for her as she stepped down on legs that were still a little wobbly from her ordeal. It felt strange to hold the skirts of her new, warm cotton dress out of the way instead of feeling the wind constantly nipping at her ankles. She made it down without tripping and then looked up as Willie opened the cottage door and led her inside.

She had stepped straight into the kitchen of her dreams, but there were no skeletons here. There was a pot-bellied little stove sitting cheerfully in the corner; a giant hearth, with a fire already laid and a little china dog gamboling on the mantelpiece; a richly patterned rug with a rocking chair right beside it. Some gnarled wooden stairs led up on the other side of the room, and a broad window at the back let in a cascade of light and a heart-lifting glimpse of a blazing oak tree in its fall colors standing amid a bare little garden.

"Oh," was all that Effie could manage.

"Is it – all right?" Willie clutched her hand nervously. "Too small?"

She turned to him, feeling her heart hammering in her chest. "Is this real?" she whispered. "Is all this really ours?"

He gathered her in his arms. "I've ordered the blue checkered curtains," he said.

Overwhelmed, she buried her face in his chest and clung to him. He stroked her freshly washed hair and kissed her head. "Are you all right?"

"Oh, Willie!" She drew back and beamed at him. "I'm more than all right. I'm…" She let him go and spun around, laughing. "I'm in a wonderful dream!"

He caught her as she spun, and then spun her himself until she giggled with giddiness. "No, you're not," he said, setting her down and gazing at her with his soft eyes. "You're in your new life, my love."

Effie gazed around at the kitchen table, and the euphoria in her heart ebbed just a little. She looked up at Willie, trying to hide her new sadness, but it was no use. He touched her chin. "What is it?" he asked.

"I…" Effie tried to smile. "I was just thinking about how… how Rose and Sadie and John would have loved this."

Willie wrapped his arms around her. "That's why we're going to hire an investigator to look for them while I'm away at sea for the next three months," he said softly.

"We are?" said Effie, staring up at him.

"Of course, we are, darling," said Willie. "We need your whole family to be here for the wedding."

Effie clung to him. "Annie loved weddings," she croaked.

"And she's going to love ours," Willie murmured.

Then he drew her in and kissed her. And she felt it all the way from her head to her toes to the very furthest reaches, the very deepest depths of her heart.

CHAPTER 15

If Effie had to liken her neighbor and friend Leticia to anything, it would be a piece of sunlight, or a hummingbird, or maybe some kind of wispy fairy – a dandelion fairy, perhaps. She flitted across the kitchen, bearing a tray of tea as if it were a dewdrop, and deposited it lightly on the table before going to perch on the chair opposite Effie's.

"Tea, darling!" she trilled. "Do try to drink it this time."

"Sorry, Leticia." Effie laughed, holding up the half-finished scarf she was knitting. "I've gotten to a difficult bit."

"Well, it looks absolutely wonderful," said Leticia. "Your Willie's going to be so impressed when he gets back and sees all the things you've learned while he was away at sea."

Effie set down her knitting and reached over the table to clasp

Leticia's soft white hand. "It's because I've had a wonderful teacher," she said.

Leticia's eyes grew misty, intensifying the wrinkles at their corners. She put her hand over Effie's and squeezed it. "Oh, my dear, it's the very least that I could do," she said.

"You are a true blessing, Leticia."

"And so are you. An old widow can grow so lonely in a cottage like this, you know," said Leticia. "You've brought so much warmth into my life these past two months."

"I would have been lonely without you," Effie admitted. "I love my cottage, but it feels so empty sometimes with Willie being away at sea."

"I'm sorry I couldn't come over yesterday. The traffic was dreadful when I went out to go shopping – although your tip about what time to go to the fish market was very useful," said Leticia, winking. "I saw you had a visitor when I got home, though."

"Yes. The investigator," said Effie.

"Has he made any progress?" asked Leticia.

"Nothing." Effie sighed. "Oh, Leticia, I don't want to be ungrateful, especially not to Willie. I've never been so happy before in all my life, I truly haven't. He has given me everything that I need, and you've been a wonderful companion, but…".

"You don't have to do any explaining to me, dear," said Leticia. "You miss your family. Nobody else is family, you know."

"I worry so much about them," said Effie. "And... and sometimes I worry about what I'll say to John even if we do ever find him. I feel I've taken so long to forgive him..." She hung her head. "Maybe it's too late."

"My darling," said Leticia, "if there is still breath in your lungs — As you learned in the Thames, even if the very breath has been taken from you, it is still never, ever too late."

Effie smiled gratefully, squeezing Leticia's hand. "You think so?"

"I know so," said Leticia. "All will be well, my dear. Just have faith." She laughed. "Now come on. It's only a month before Willie will come home, and then that nice warm scarf will need to be ready for him."

***

EFFIE HUNG ON TIGHTLY TO LETICIA'S HAND AS THEY walked down toward the docks. Spring had filled the air with fragrance back in the row of cottages where she'd been living so snugly for the past three months, but here it smelled as it always did: of fish. The smell made her skin crawl, and she moved a little closer to Leticia as a gaggle of sailors walked past them, laughing uproariously.

"Don't be frightened," said Leticia, squeezing her hand. "They won't touch a lady like you – not when I'm here with my cane, in any case."

"Do you..." Effie swallowed. "Do you think he's really here?"

"Of course, he's here, love," said Leticia. "Look. There's his ship right over there, the *Hazelnut*. We'll see him in..."

The crowd burst apart, and Willie was rushing out from amongst them, his boots stomping on the cobbles, his white shirt blowing open to show that glimpse of chest hair, his eyes shining. "Effie!" he cried.

She couldn't speak. She just let him sweep her up into his arms and spin her around and around. She buried her face into the warmth and softness of his hair, allowing the smell of the sea to surround her. She wasn't sure if she wanted to laugh or cry or just curl up and sleep forever in the safety of his arms. He cupped her face in his hands and smothered her in kisses. "My love," he said with a gasp. "You're here."

"Of course, I'm here!" Effie laughed up at him, wrapping her arms around his neck. "Where else would I be? I'm marrying you in just three weeks."

Willie beamed, and his smile filled her entire world. "Yes, you are," he said. "And your family will be there."

Effie felt her smile falter. "Oh, Willie," she began, "you've tried so hard, but—"

"Effie." Willie gripped her arms. "The investigator. He's found John."

Effie felt as though her world had suddenly stood still. *"What?"*

"It was all so sudden. Apparently, a young man named John Wilson, the right age and the right description, has just opened a bakery across town," said Willie. "The investigator came across the advertisement and thinks it's probably him, just two days ago. Knowing I was coming back from the voyage, he decided to meet me at the docks rather than tell you, not wanting to give you too much of a shock."

Effie could feel her throat tightening. She struggled to take a few deep breaths, clinging to Willie's arms to keep the dizziness at bay. "What... what will we do?"

"First, we'll go home," he said. "And I'll kiss my lovely bride-to-be, and we'll have a cup of tea and calm down. And then I'm going to take you to see your brother, my love." Willie kissed her. "And everything will be all right."

She smiled at him, even though her insides felt shaky. "You know, Willie, I never believed that," she said. "But when you say it, I have to."

"That's because it's true," said Willie. "Now come, my special lady, let's go home."

The spring evening was crisp and frosty, but Effie didn't feel it, her feet in neat little boots, a fur coat wrapped around her shoulders and a woolly muffler over her hands. Willie tucked her hat down a little further over her ears and wrapped an arm around her shoulders. "Are you cold, my love?" he asked.

"No," said Effie.

"But you're shaking."

She was shaking, and the cold had nothing to do with it. Staring across the little market square, she couldn't take her eyes off the bakery. The light inside was golden in the cool blues and grays of the evening, casting yellow squares on the stone outside. She could see figures moving to and fro within, but they were just a little too far away for her to make out their faces. The shelves were filled with wonderful golden things, and the smell reached her where she stood, making her mouth water.

"Effie?" Willie prompted.

"I – I'm scared," Effie whispered. "What if it's not him? What if..." She paused. "What if it *is* him, and I don't know what to say?"

"Then don't say anything," said Willie. "Just be there."

"I don't know if he can forgive me," said Effie. "I don't know if I really have forgiven him, even though I've tried."

"You've found him, my love," said Willie. He squeezed her tight. "That's a good start."

"I hope so," she whispered.

"Should I come with you?"

Effie shook her head slowly. How she wanted him to, but she said, "No. This... this is something I have to do by myself."

He kissed her forehead. "Then go, beloved, and my heart goes with you."

She felt very small and alone as she walked across the square toward the neat little building, and she couldn't quite make herself look up at the sign across the top. She couldn't really read yet, but when she'd stood across the square, she'd made out something that looked like her last name – WILSON, which she knew how to write – and then something else that began with the letter J. She didn't know how she could be more afraid and nervous as she tucked her head down and walked in rapid little steps to the door of the bakery just as it was drawn gently shut.

She stopped, confused, her heart stinging. Had John recognized her and shut her out already?

Lifting her eyes to the door, she saw the sign hanging on it said something that didn't look like OPEN. CLOSED, she supposed.

A face appeared at the window on her left. Before she could

react, it vanished again, and the door opened. "I'm sorry, ma'am," it said. It was musical, fluting, playful. "We've just shut, but I can still help you if you need something?"

Effie couldn't believe her ears. She looked up straight into the face of a beautiful, grown-up Rose whose red locks fell in luxurious curls around her shoulders, framing a face with pink cheeks and shining brown eyes. The eyes suddenly widened, filling with tears. Rose lifted her hand to her lips.

Effie couldn't speak.

They stared at one another for a second that seemed to quiver on the precipice of danger. Then Rose lowered her hands and croaked out a name.

"S-Sadie?" she managed.

Incredibly, Sadie appeared behind her sister, tall and willowy as ever, her black hair hanging to her very hips. Her somber eyes settled on Effie's face and lit up more brightly than she'd ever seen them do before.

"Effie!" she cried, pushing Rose aside and lunging forward, and the next minute Effie was holding her in her arms – Sadie, one of the sisters she'd lost two years ago, safely wrapped in Effie's embrace. Rose's arms were thrown around both of them, and her sisters were crying, and Effie was holding on to them with all of her might even though it was harder than she remembered to fit her arms around them both at once.

"Effie! Effie!" They were sobbing together. "Oh, Effie, you've come looking for us!"

Effie's own eyes were dry, although she could feel the wall of her tears trembling. She stepped back, gripping their hands, studying them both. "My darlings," she cried. "You look so well! But how... and why..."

"It was John, Effie," said Sadie. "It was all John. He scoured London for us. He searched high and low until he found us in a terrible, terrible workhouse where we'd been taken."

"John?" said Effie.

A figure appeared in the doorway, eclipsing the warm light from within, and Effie looked up. He was standing there behind the girls, his arms folded. His hair had been cut short, and he was so much bigger than Effie remembered, but his eyes were the same as always. Strong, yet there was a softness in them.

"John," Effie croaked. "You... you found our sisters."

He took one giant step forward and held out his arms, but then hesitating as if held back by an invisible chain.

"Now I've found all my sisters," he said, his voice deep and different, yet as warm and sweet and sturdy as the smell of fresh-baked bread that rolled off his crisp white apron.

The wall of tears shattered, his voice obliterating it, crushing it to dust, scattering it to the four winds and making it vanish.

The tears cascaded out of her, and she cried, and he wrapped her in his arms, and she finally felt something like whole again.

※

The morning had been one of so much hustle and bustle that Effie felt that these few seconds outside the church were the first moments of quiet that she'd been able to have all day. Even now, it felt as though all of her insides were trembling with something that was so far beyond joy and excitement that it felt like she was flying, or skipping from one sunbeam to the other, perhaps. She felt like there was a bird beating its free wings in her chest where her heart should be, and that it would lift her up and take her soaring high into the sky if she gave it half a chance.

She put a hand on her chest, trying to calm it. Her palm rested against white satin so soft it felt as though she was wearing duck down. Looking down at her lap, she could almost see her face in the shining fabric. She'd glimpsed into a mirror a few minutes ago as Leticia finished putting up the last of her hair, pinning it in place with a single great white rose that shone like a full moon amid her black hair. Leticia had been crying happy tears, Effie had been crying happy tears, Rose had been crying happy tears and Sadie had been sharply cajoling them all to keep it together.

She could hear them coming around the corner now, and in a

moment they both appeared, resplendent in the brightest blue. Rose's eyes were dancing. She put her bouquet of forget-me-nots into one hand to seize Effie's.

"Come on, Effie!" she cried. "Get ready. Sadie and I are about to go down the aisle."

Sadie laughed. "Don't hurry her so, Rosie," she said. "She's even more excited for her own wedding than you are as it is!"

Effie gave a shaky smile. "Do I look all right, girls?"

Sadie gripped Effie's hands and pulled her gently to her feet, giving her a sober look. "Effie, my dear sister," she said, "Willie fell in love with you when you were a street urchin, but when you step into that church, he's going to think he's marrying an angel."

Effie blinked back tears. Now that the wall had been broken, the tears came so easily these days. "Thank you," she croaked.

Rose kissed her cheek. "I'll see you when you're *Mrs.* Green," she said, giggling.

A fanfare of organ music blared inside the church. Sadie gave Effie's hands a last squeeze and let them go. "We love you," she said.

The ushers pulled the church doors open, and Sadie and Rose walked down the aisle side by side, clutching their matching bouquets. For a moment, Effie couldn't take her eyes off them. Somehow those two grubby, starving, frightened little girls had grown into two lovely women, their every stride matching as they walked into the church ahead of her, and they took her breath away.

A discreetly waving hand caught her eye in the pews. They were quite empty, but to Effie, that church filled her entire world. It was John. He was beaming, his large frame squeezed into a neat black suit, and the brotherly love in his eyes had changed her world forever.

They were all here – all four of them. Effie closed her eyes for a moment, aware that everyone in the church was watching her where she stood in her gleaming white dress, and she remembered a small child with the brightest blue eyes in all the world. She remembered a smile as bright as if the stars had all been trapped in her pinched, pale little face. Reaching up to her own face, Effie traced her fingertips across her chin, feeling that light touch again.

You look so beautiful. Annie's voice rang in her mind as clearly as if the past six years had never happened. Effie felt a tear slip out of her eye and run hotly down her cheek. She looked down at the aisle and pictured a little girl who would never grow old, a little girl all in white who had grown her angel wings. Annie was dancing, laughing, smiling, holding out two healthy hands to her.

I love weddings, she was singing. *I love weddings.*

"And I love you," Effie whispered under her breath.

Only then did she raise her eyes to the front of the church, and he was standing there, her beautiful future, her lifesaver, her world. His eyes held everything she had ever wanted. Effie took a deep breath and let everything fall back behind her, and she began to walk down the aisle.

The End

CONTINUE READING...

THANK you for reading **Abandoned Wharf Sisters! Are you wondering what to read next?** Why not read ***A Desolate Christmas? Here's a sneak peek for you:***

Mama's eyes were the same shade of amber as her hair, except that the light scattered a little differently inside them. Staring up into them, Lena thought they were the same colour as her favourite milk chocolates. Maybe a little richer; and milk chocolate didn't make the candlelight come to life the way Mama's eyes did.

"Mama, you have such pretty eyes." Lena reached up with her hands, laying one on each of Mama's soft cheeks. "I love them."

Mama smiled. "I love your eyes too, Lena." She reached out to touch the tip of Lena's nose. "They're the bluest of blues."

Lena giggled. "Your eyes look like chocolate."

Mama scooped Lena up into her arms, planting a kiss on her forehead as she sat down in the armchair by the little bed. Lena snuggled into her lap, placing her freshly washed head on Mama's shoulders. "How come some people have blue eyes and some people have brown eyes?" Lena asked, trying to hold back the wave of sleepiness that was threatening to overwhelm her.

"Well, it all depends what the fairies put in them," said Mama.

"So the fairies put chocolate in your eyes?" asked Lena in wonder.

"They must have." Mama nuzzled Lena's cheek, then kissed it.

"But what did they put in my eyes?"

Mama sat back in the armchair, thinking about the question. It was late, and the fire in the hearth was crackling warmly, filling the nursery with its dancing light. The gas lamps on the walls seemed bland by comparison. Lena listened to Mama's voice, gazing at the little rocking-horses that adorned the wallpaper of her room.

"I think the fairies went all the way up into the summer sky," said Mama. "They made a little fire out of their magic, and they melted a corner of the sky and put it in a teacup. Then they came to you when you were a baby and poured the pretty sky right into your eyes." Mama reached for Lena's hair, twirling one of her ringlets around her finger. "And while they were about it, they spun a few rays of sunshine into hair for you on a spinning wheel."

Lena giggled. "Tell me another story, Mama," she said.

"It's bedtime, my darling."

"Please, Mama? Pretty please," Lena begged. "It doesn't have to be a long one."

"Oh, all right, then." Mama cuddled her closer. "Do you want to hear another story about fairies?"

Visit Here to Continue Reading:

http://www.ticahousepublishing.com/victorian-romance.html

THANKS FOR READING

If you love Victorian Romance, **Click Here**

https://victorian.subscribemenow.com/

to hear about all **New Faye Godwin Romance Releases! I will let you know as soon as they become available!**

Thank you, Friends! If you enjoyed ***Abandoned Wharf Sisters,*** would you kindly take a couple minutes to leave a positive review on Amazon? It only takes a moment, and positive reviews truly make a difference. Thank you so much! I appreciate it!

Much love,

Faye Godwin

MORE FAYE GODWIN VICTORIAN ROMANCES!

We love rich, dramatic Victorian Romances and have a library of Faye Godwin titles just for you! (Remember that ALL of Faye's Victorian titles can be downloaded FREE with Kindle Unlimited!)

VISIT HERE to discover Faye's Complete Collection of Victorian Romance:

https://ticahousepublishing.com/victorian-romance.html

ABOUT THE AUTHOR

Faye Godwin has been fascinated with Victorian Romance since she was a teen. After reading every Victorian Romance in her public library, she decided to start writing them herself —which she's been doing ever since. Faye lives with her husband and young son in England. She loves to travel throughout her country, dreaming up new plots for her romances. She's delighted to join the Tica House Publishing family and looks forward to getting to know her readers.

contact@ticahousepublishing.com